Staffordshire Library and Information Service

KT-465-685

Please return or renew or by the last date shown

KINVER		
18. APR		
0 8 FEB 2019		

If not required by other readers, this item may be renewed
in person, by post or telephone, online or by email.
To renew, either the book or ticket are required

**24 Hour Renewal Line
0845 33 00 740**

Staffordshire
County Council

PROUD JOURNEY

FROG JOURNEY

PROUD JOURNEY

Wayne D. Overholser

GUNSMOKE

First published in the US by Doubleday

This hardback edition 2012
by AudioGO Ltd
by arrangement with
Golden West Literary Agency

ISBN 978 1 445 82406 2

British Library Cataloguing in Publication Data available.

Printed and bound in Great Britain by
MPG Books Group Limited

The westbound train had followed the Arkansas for miles. Now it slowed, for Canon City, Colorado, was just ahead. The whistle cried out shrilly, the bell clanged with monotonous, metallic clacking as the train rolled past the first corrals and shacks at the edge of town, the little engine laying a plume of smoke all the way back to the rear car.

People began to stir, for, in this year of 1879, this was the end of the ribbon of steel. The passengers who were going beyond Canon City would stay the night here and in the morning would take the stagecoach to Leadville, or to Gunnison across the range. From Gunnison some would go to the Los Pinos Indian Agency, or on to the mining camps in the San Juan beyond the agency.

Rather than think about the tiresome journey to the agency, Dave Rand had amused himself for the last hour by guessing where each of the twenty-odd passengers who occupied the car were going and why. Most of them were men, and with one exception he thought he could identify them. They were gamblers, ranchers, greenhorns from the East, or miners. The exception was the dark-complexioned man who sat across the aisle from Dave.

The man was about thirty. He was almost as tall as Dave, with broad shoulders that threatened to break the seams of the coat of his blue serge suit. His black mustache was the bristly kind, his dark eyes sharp and probing, and he was, Dave thought, handsome in a rough-featured way. He might be a miner, or a freighter, or possibly a businessman, maybe one who dealt in mining supplies. He wasn't a soft-handed counterjumper. Dave was sure of that.

Of the five women in the coach, Dave felt certain he had mentally identified four. Two were undoubtedly fancy women, occupying a seat by themselves in the rear of the car. Two others were harried mothers with small children, probably wives on their way to join husbands who had gone on ahead to find a place for them to live. But the fifth woman who sat two seats in front of Dave was even harder to fit into one of Dave's pigeonholes than the dark-complexioned man.

She was tall, blond and blue-eyed, the skin of her face tanned much darker than was usual with blond women. Dave guessed she was twenty-two or -three. Her features were good, her figure excellent even in the loose-fitting gray suit she wore. She was, he decided, a very attractive woman and one he would like to know.

Dave shrugged, thinking he would probably never see her again, and glanced out of the window at the barren hills north of the river. It was his kind of country, big and empty and challenging, and he felt as if he had come home. He promised himself he would never go East again to live, then smiled at the foolishness of the promise, for he knew full well that a man was seldom in command of his destiny.

The conductor poked his head into the coach, calling, "Canon City. End of the line. Canon City."

Dave rose and pulled his suitcase from the luggage rack as the coach jerked to a jolting stop. The blond girl was struggling with her suitcases as Dave moved along the aisle to her. He said, "Let me help you." The instant the words were out of his mouth, he realized that the dark-complexioned man was standing beside him and had said almost the same thing.

As the two men glared at each other, the girl looked at them and laughed. Her frank amusement melted the irritation in Dave and he laughed in spite of himself. The dark-complexioned man scowled, then he grinned and the tension was broken.

"I have two heavy suitcases and one small valise," she said, "and they were just about more than I could handle when I got on at Denver. Now I have more help than I can use.''

"The good things of life are seldom distributed equally,'' Dave said as he pulled one of the girl's suitcases from the rack. "I'll divide with you, friend. We'll each take one and that'll make us both happy.''

"A philosopher," the dark-complexioned man said in disgust. "You never know what you're going to run into on a train.''

Dave followed the girl along the aisle and out of the car, the other man coming behind them. The instant Dave stepped to the cinders beside the track, he sensed that something had happened. The crowd that had flowed out of the coaches was milling about. The men were shouting at each other, the women with the children were crying, the two fancy women who stood apart from the others looked around uncertainly as if not sure what they should do.

The blond girl turned to Dave. "What is it?"

"I don't know." He couldn't make out more than an occasional word or flurry of words: "The Utes . . ." "Nathan Meeker's dead by now . . ." "Thornburgh's pinned down with his whole command.''

A man wearing a green eyeshade ran along the track toward the depot. Dave set the suitcases down and stepped in front of the man, asking, "What happened?''

"The White River Utes are on the warpath," the man said hurriedly. "Major Thomas Thornburgh was taking some soldiers to the agency to protect the agent, Nathan Meeker, but he never got there. The red devils ambushed him on Milk Creek. His whole command might be wiped out by now.''

"What about Meeker and the rest of the whites who were at the agency?''

"Nobody knows," the man said. "You staying in Canon City?''

"No, I'm going to the Los Pinos Agency.''

"Take my advice and don't do it," the man warned. "The minute you get on the other side of the range you're in Indian country and you'll lose your hair.''

He rushed on toward the depot. Dave stared at his back until he disappeared in the crowd, knowing that what somebody had said about Meeker being dead was probably right if the White River Utes had mustered up enough courage to fight the United States Army.

A man on the other side of the blond girl was saying, "The rest of the Utes will go after some scalps now. They'll cross the reservation line and wipe Gunnison out."

"All I can say is that I'm damned glad I didn't get no farther," another said. "I'm taking the next train back to Pueblo."

The blond girl had been listening. Now she turned to Dave. "What does it mean? I was going to Ouray, but I'm wondering if they'll stop the stagecoaches."

"I doubt it," Dave said, "but unless I miss my guess they'll be running empty." He motioned toward the crowd. "Funny how panic spreads when something like this sets it off. Before they get done, they'll have every white man within fifty miles of the reservation killed and scalped."

"I guess they just enjoy scaring each other," the dark-complexioned man said. "Same as sitting around a camp-fire on a foggy night telling ghost stories."

The girl's gaze clung to Dave's face. "You don't think it's as bad as they're saying?"

"Not for this part of the state," Dave answered. "There won't be any trouble with the Uncompahgre Utes. Ouray is their chief and he's always been friendly with the whites. I don't see any reason for him to change."

"Let's go get our hotel rooms," the dark-complexioned man said. "No sense standing here listening to this scare talk. If the stage goes out in the morning, I'll be on it."

Dave picked up the suitcases and turned toward the hotel, the other two walking beside him, the three long shadows moving across the dust with them. The girl was quite pale, Dave saw, and he wondered why she was going to Ouray. At least he knew something about her now.

He felt her sway beside him and, glancing at her, he sensed that she was staring at the hotel ahead of them but he doubted that she saw it. She was trying to decide about going on or staying, he thought, and found himself hoping that she would be on the stage in the morning, partly because he would enjoy her company, but mostly because he would be disappointed in her if she was influenced by the contagion of fear which had swept through the train passengers.

They entered the hotel lobby and set the luggage down. Dave watched the girl sign *Sharon Morgan* and add *Denver, Colorado.* The dark-complexioned man took the pen, dipped it into the ink, and wrote *Vince Kelso, Pueblo, Colorado,* and handed the pen to Dave. He wrote his name and gave Washington, D.C. as his address.

"May I have the key to my room?" Sharon asked.

"We don't have no keys," the clerk said. "If you have any trouble, holler. You take room ten, ma'am." He turned the register and looked at Kelso's name. "Number twelve, Mr. Kelso." He frowned when he saw Dave's address. "Another goddamned politician," he muttered, then shrugged. "You take fourteen."

The crowd was streaming toward the hotel from the depot, still excited and still panicky. Dave asked, "You figure the stage will go out in the morning?"

"It'll go to Cleora anyway," the clerk said. "We got the word on the wire about an hour before the train got in. Folks were a mite jumpy at first, but soon as we thought about it, we knowed we wouldn't have no trouble here. You'd be smart to hang onto your room, mister. It's better'n you'll find in Cleora. If you go on over the range from there, you're a dead man."

"What time does the stage leave?"

"Seven. Dining room opens at six."

Dave nodded as he picked up the suitcases and turned toward the stairs. Sharon and Kelso had already reached the hall above. He took the steps two at a time and, following Sharon into her room, set her suitcase beside the one Kelso had carried.

"Thank you very much," the girl said.

"My pleasure." Dave touched the brim of his hat. "Maybe we'll see you at breakfast, Miss Morgan."

"Perhaps you will," she said.

Dave stepped into the hall and closed the door. Kelso was looking at him speculatively. He said in a low tone, "Ten dollars she's on the stage in the morning."

"I'm a gambling man," Dave said, "but I'm not one to bet against something I believe." He opened the door of his room and put his suitcase down. "I'll buy you a drink, Kelso."

"I'll take you up on that as soon as I get rid of this bag," Kelso said.

Dave turned toward the stairs, the racket of talk a shrill sound that flowed up from the lobby. He wondered where the two fancy women would spend the night, and where the women with the children were going and how long they would stay here in Canon City. Then, as Kelso joined him, he thought about Sharon Morgan, attractive and self-possessed. She had not been stampeded by the scare talk, and in Dave Rand's opinion, she had more courage than most of the men who were milling around the lobby and talking about killing Utes.

He had noticed that she was wearing neither an engagement nor a wedding ring, but still she might be going to Ouray to meet the man she was going to marry. Then, for no reason that made good sense, he hoped she wasn't.

Dave spent most of the night playing poker, but he was up before six and having breakfast with Kelso when Sharon Morgan entered the dining room. Dave rose and pulled back a chair for her.

"Good morning," he said as she crossed the room to them. "Are you ready for a rough ride?"

"Good morning," she said, smiling. "I'm as ready as I ever will be."

Kelso rose and said, "Good morning," and dropped back into his chair.

The waitress came to the table, took Sharon's order, and left, then Sharon asked, "Is there any news?"

"No, but I did hear a little more of the story," Dave said. "A courier got through the Indian lines and made a fast ride to Rawlins. He sent the news on the wire and I understand that Colonel Merritt is putting a relief party together, but it will take time."

"And while that time is being taken, Thornburgh's men may all be killed," she said, the good humor leaving her face.

"That's right," Dave agreed. "In fact, Thornburgh was killed the first day of the fighting. Captain Payne was in command when the courier left."

"I never heard of him," the girl said, and added angrily, "from now on every schoolboy will know the name Thornburgh and it will go down in the history books along with Custer. I hate every Indian in the United States."

"You must have a powerful reason to go through the reservation to Ouray if you feel that way about Indians," Dave said.

7

Her order came and she started to eat. Dave thought she
was going to ignore his remark. He didn't blame her, for it
was not one he had a right to make. Still, he was irritated
by what he considered her intolerance. To hate all Indians
because one small bank of White River Utes had gone
berserk was unreasonable.

"No," she said finally. "I don't have a powerful reason
for going through the reservation to Ouray. It's just that
I'm planning to establish a millinery business and the
sooner I get it started the better. Besides, you never know
about winter in the mountains. I'd like to make the trip and
get settled before the weather turns bad."

"Same with me," Kelso said. "I'm looking for work
and I've got the promise of a job in Ouray if I show up
before someone else gets it."

"What kind of work?" Dave asked.

"Freighting," Kelso said.

Dave finished his breakfast and pushed his plate back. "I
apologize if I seem to be prying, Miss Morgan," he
began, "but I can't understand the urgency in getting to
Ouray before winter sets in just to start a millinery business. Not when an Indian war is being threatened."

"You are prying," she said, "but it's natural after what
I said about my feeling toward Indians. I guess I am a little
frightened, but if you men don't think there is any danger,
and if the stage company doesn't, either, and I'm sure it
doesn't or the stage wouldn't be going through, I don't see
any good reason why I should sit here and spend money in
a Canon City hotel that I could use to get my business
started in Ouray."

"That makes sense," Dave admitted. "The man I stopped
beside the train tried to scare us, then the clerk here in
the hotel did the same. I guess folks hereabouts want to
keep all the business they can."

Kelso flung out an arm to call attention to the nearly
empty dining room. "Looks like they're keeping it. There
sure ain't gonna be a big crowd on the stage."

"There won't be many people coming in on the train
until this is settled." Dave glanced at the pendulum clock

by the door. "We'd better move or we won't be on the stage, either. Is your luggage ready to bring down?"

"I didn't open the suitcases," she said. "They're just inside the door."

"We'll fetch them down for you," Dave said.

The stage was waiting by the time Dave and Kelso reached the boardwalk in front of the hotel. A minute or so later Sharon joined them. Dave gave her a hand up and then stepped into the coach and sat down beside her. Kelso took the seat opposite them. As Dave expected, they were the only passengers.

The driver climbed to the high seat, released the brake, and yelled as his whip cracked with pistol sharpness over the horses. The coach started with a lurch that threw Sharon against Dave.

"I'm sorry," she said as she drew back into her corner.

"I don't mind," he said, smiling.

"The good things of life are seldom distributed equally," Kelso remarked smugly.

"A philosopher," Dave said as if disgusted. "You never know what you're going to run into in a stage-coach."

"You remind me that it's my turn to pry," the girl said. "Do you have an urgent reason to go to the agency?"

"I have to," he said. "It's my job. I'm a writer for a Washington newspaper and I'm out here to do a series of articles on the various Indian agencies in Colorado. Funny thing how people in the East are interested in Indians." He laughed shortly. "It's also funny how fate deals your hand for you sometimes. If I had gone to the .White River Agency which I had originally planned to do, I'd probably be lying dead beside Nathan Meeker's body right now."

She lowered her gaze to her hands that were folded on the reticule that lay on her lap. She said, "Yes, I often wonder about things like that."

They were silent then, the stage starting the steep climb west of town to swing around the Royal Gorge of the Arkansas, a plum that had been fought over by the Denver & Rio Grande and the Sante Fe railroads because it was the only water-level avenue through which the traffic with the rich mining country around Leadville could flow, but it was too narrow to permit the construction of a wagon road.

The horses labored to the top, then the road swung back down to the river, brakes screaming as the coach made the sharp descent. For a time after that they paralleled the river until the sheer rock walls closed in once more and they had to climb to the rim again. That was the pattern of the day's travel until, near evening, the stage finally wheeled out of the tight-walled canyon to the flat that held the town of Cleora, the October sun a full circle above the Continental Divide to the west.

Dave had slept much of the time since they left Canon City, but he was awake now, relieved that the day's travel was behind them. He could not, he told himself, have stood it for another mile. Stagecoaches, he had discovered years ago, were not made for long-legged men.

The stage pulled up in front of a two-story log building that was, according to the sign, the CLEORA HOTEL. Dave opened the door and stepped down and stretched, feeling as if he had just escaped from a straitjacket. He reached up and gave Sharon a hand, then Kelso stepped out, rubbing his buttocks.

"It's enough to give a man calluses," he said. "All three of us are crazy to ride this thing three days straight hand running."

Sharon kept her hand in Dave's for a moment as she swayed uncertainly, her eyes closed. She opened them and stepped away from him, embarrassed. "I'm sorry," she said. "I was all right till I stood up and then the world began going around."

"You just need to change your sea legs for land legs." Dave climbed to the boot, asking, "You want all your luggage?"

"Just the little valise," she said.

He found it and stepped back to the ground and stood beside her as the coach lumbered on past the hotel. He said, "I'll carry it in."

"Well, judging from the size of the crowd, we won't

have no trouble getting rooms,'' Kelso said, ''but it'll be different in Gunnison tomorrow.''

''You all there is?'' a thin-faced man asked.

He had stepped out of the hotel and now stood glaring at them as if he held them personally accountable for the lack of business.

''We're it,'' Dave said. ''The news caught up with us at Canon City.''

''Dirty, stinking red devils,'' the man said angrily. ''It ain't enough for 'em to be fed and given presents and then keep white men off some of the best land in Colorado. Now they've got to raise hell and scare folks into staying away, and me with supper enough for more'n a dozen people.''

Dave wanted to slap the man's face. What he had just said was typical of the attitude of too many Colorado people. For months the slogan, ''The Utes must go,'' had echoed from one end of the state to the other, but Dave was cynic enough to feel certain that the only motive behind the push to move the Indians out of Colorado was the selfish hope that opening up the big reservation would make rich men out of many who now were poor. He wondered if this greedy, skinny man standing in front of him and worrying about his unsold suppers had felt the slightest regret over the death of Major Thornburgh and those of his command who had gone down with him.

Dave pinned his gaze on the hotel man's face and he hit him with his words as if he were using a bull whip, ''You've got some business right here that's waiting, mister. You'd better take care of it.''

The man straightened, his eyes narrowing. ''You figure you're a tough hand, friend?''

''I don't know as to that,'' Dave said, ''but I do know we're tired and we're hungry, so take care of it instead of cussing the Indians.''

For a moment the man stood there, his gaze raking Dave's tall figure as if debating whether to make anything out of it or not, then he shrugged. ''Sign the register. Take your pick of the rooms upstairs.''

He stepped back into the lobby and swung around and disappeared into the bar. "A friendly host," Kelso said.

"Yeah, real friendly," Dave agreed, and set the girl's valise on the floor.

They signed the register and climbed the stairs, Sharon taking the front corner room. She looked around at the bare walls and the single window with it green shade and the upended box that held a candle and a white pitcher that was filled with water. A basin was on the floor beside a slop jar. A bed covered by two dingy blankets was the only other piece of furniture in the room.

She looked at Dave, a small smile coming to her lips. "And I thought the room in Canon City was a poor one."

He glanced at the door and saw that it had no lock. He said, "It may be a little rough around here before morning. I'll take the next room so I'll be handy if you have any trouble."

"Thank you," she said gratefully. "I was very brave this morning, but I guess I'm not as brave as I thought I was."

"You'll do," he said. "Kelso and I will wait downstairs for you and we can have supper together. "

"I'd appreciate that," she said.

He stepped into the hall and closed the door, noting that Kelso had taken the room across from her. Dave said, "I told her we'd wait to eat with her."

"Good," Kelso said. "Rand, this is a hell of a place for a lady, and the more I see of her, the surer I am that she's a lady."

Dave smiled, remembering how he'd had difficulty on the train cataloguing both Kelso and the girl. He had been right about Kelso, but he had not guessed that Sharon was on her way to Ouray to start a millinery business.

"She'll make out," Dave said.

"Sure she will," Kelso said quickly. "If she was the complaining kind, we'd have heard from her today."

Dave stepped into his room and closed the door. He took off his shirt and undershirt and, pouring water into the basin, soaped himself from the waist up, rinsed, and dried. He dressed and, taking a comb from his pocket, ran it through his thick brown hair, parting it on the left side and giving it a high roach on the right. When he stepped into the hall, he found Vince Kelso waiting for him.

Dave paused in the lobby to light a cigar, then followed Kelso to the porch and stood there in companionable silence, relishing the taste and fragrance of the Havana. It was a good cigar, one from a box he had bought in Denver. He had paid more for it than he could afford, but smoking was his one luxury and he did not regret the price. It would be a long time before he would have the opportunity to buy another box.

He watched the daylight fade and become dusk. The great peaks of the Continental Divide to the west, Mount Shavano and the others, turned dark against the lighter sky. They stood out clearly for a time, reminding Dave of a jagged edge of a sheet of black paper held against a dying light. In the morning they would give an entirely different appearance when the first slanted rays of the sun caught the very tips of the peaks. This was a sort of miracle which he had witnessed many times when he had lived in Colorado.

He glanced at the Sangre de Cristo range to the south and saw that the last of the sunlight, finding a break somewhere in the range to the west, was painting the upper slopes with an unbelievably bright tint. Then the light died and the ridges turned black. He thought they would probably seem menacing to people like Sharon Morgan who were not used to living in the mountains. He wondered how she would feel in Ouray which lay in a bowl almost surrounded by tall peaks.

Dave pulled on his cigar and watched the smoke cloud disintegrate in the chill evening air. Everything was transient, he mused, whether it was a cloud of cigar smoke or a man's life. Each breath brought him closer to death, but it did not change his reason for being or his beliefs about God and man, or the causes which he considered worth dying for. He gave this last thought some attention and decided he was wrong, that causes, like sunsets, were transient.

He heard Kelso whistle softly, and say, "Let's go put the feed bag on. She's ready."

Dave turned to see Sharon standing in the lobby waiting for them. She stood very tall and straight, carrying herself with what seemed to Dave a kind of regal bearing. She had changed from the gray traveling suit to a marine blue dress with a tight skirt that was ankle length.

He tossed his cigar stub away and saw the sparks explode into a red spray as it struck the hard dirt of the yard. He followed Kelso and Sharon through the lobby and into the dining room. He had seen many fine-looking and well-dressed women in Washington, he told himself, but none equalled Sharon Morgan in either grace or beauty.

Kelso reached a table ahead of Dave and pulled a chair back for Sharon, glancing at Dave in triumph. Sharon said, "Thank you," and sat down.

"The dress is perfect for you," Dave said as he took a chair to her right. "If I were an artist, I would want to paint you."

She gave him a searching look to see if he were being facetious, he thought. She apparently decided he wasn't, for she said, "It's very kind of you to say so, Mr. Rand."

"Well," Kelso said with visible irritation, "I don't have a slick tongue which I heard the East develops in a man, but I know a pretty woman when I see one."

"Now we have a connoisseur of feminine pulchritude as well as a philosopher," Dave said. "You never know what you'll run into in a hotel dining room."

"If you want to go outside . . ." Kelso began.

"No, I don't want to go outside," Dave said, glancing at the waitress who had come to their table. "Let's see if they have anything fit to eat."

After taking their order, the waitress left. Kelso said, still angry, "You were using some fancy words I didn't know. I thought that if we went outside you could explain them to me."

"Later," Dave said, realizing that he had needled Kelso in a tender spot and he regretted it.

Sharon was embarrassed. She glanced from one to the other, then asked, "Am I missing something?"

"You're just watching a natural law at work," Dave said, smiling. "It always happens when two homely males compete for the attention of a beautiful woman."

"Oh," she said. "I suppose I'm honored."

"Certainly," Dave assured her, "although I will admit I have wondered if our attention will be wasted. Perhaps there is a man waiting for you in Ouray, a childhood sweetheart who struck it rich, then wrote to you and asked you to come to Ouray and promised he would build you a mansion with a mansard roof and gold doorknobs."

She laughed and shook her head. "I'm afraid not. I'll be lucky to find a man who will manage my suitcases when I get to Ouray."

"I'm curious," Dave said. "Why did you pick Ouray?"

"No good reason," she answered. "I just thought that it was a new mining camp and I'd find more business there than I would in an older town where there was probably a millinery shop already."

"Sure," Kelso said, his good humor returning. "Same with me. A new camp means opportunity if a man's got a little push. I guess it's the same with women." His eyes narrowed, and he added, "A newspaperman is on the go all the time, ain't he? You'll spend a few days at Los Pinos and then go somewhere else."

"I'm a rolling stone if that's what you mean," Dave said, "and I haven't gathered much moss. I will be here for a while, though. I have to stop a day or so at Major Leslie's place on the Cimarron. It's inside the reservation and I understand that he is better acquainted with the Indian problem than anyone else in Colorado. After that I'll be at the agency for some time." He looked at Sharon, smiling. "Then I'll come to Ouray and see how many hats you've sold."

"That's a promise," she said. "I'll expect you."

Kelso was looking at the girl, too. He said, "You may not have as much business as you expect. A new camp like Ouray don't have many good women."

Sharon was momentarily embarrassed, then she said lightly, "I'm not above doing business with bad women, Mr. Kelso."

The waitress came with their food. The steak was tough, the biscuits hard, the coffee bitter. Dave and Kelso were able to eat, but Sharon did little more than push her food around her plate.

Presently Sharon put her fork down. "I'll have to ask to be excused. I guess I'm tired. I didn't sleep very much in Canon City last night."

After she left, Dave lighted a cigar, his gaze on Kelso. He said, "I'm sorry. I wasn't trying to show off."

Kelso leaned back and rolled a cigarette. "Looked to me like you was. I didn't come from no rich family like you probably done, and I don't have much book learning, but I ain't backing up any. I'm going to Ouray, too, and by God, I'll give you a run for your money with her."

"I expect you will." Dave paused, thinking of his stern boyhood and the little formal schooling that he'd had, but decided there was no point in his saying anything about it to Kelso. Instead, he said lightly, "Well, they say everything's fair in love and war."

Kelso reached into his vest pocket for a match. He said, "It's too soon to tell how any of us feel, but I'll tell you one thing. If it turns out to be love, it sure as hell is going to be war." He struck the match and held the flame to his cigarette. He blew out a great cloud of smoke, then he said, "She made a mistake coming out here. I've lived in Colorado for twenty years, and I've been in most of the mining camps. They're filled with toughs. I hate to see her bucking the kind of life she'll be up against."

"I've got a hunch she's the kind of woman who can take care of herself," Dave said.

Kelso shook his head. "Coming from the East, you don't know what it's like."

"I've seen a little rough life," Dave said. "I was raised in Colorado."

Kelso's face showed his surprise. "I had the notion all the time you were a greenhorn who'd strayed off his pasture."

Dave shook his head. "You might say I'm coming back to the pasture."

Kelso rose. "I'll buy you a drink. Let's see if they've

got anything better'n the liquid lightning they usually sell in a place like this."

Dave rose and walked into the barroom with Kelso. "I hope the grub in Gunnison is better'n this."

"We might not get any," Kelso said. "It's a new camp, and from what I hear, there ain't much in the way of accommodations. All the prospectors will be heading for town with this Indian scare like it is."

"We'll find a bed for Sharon if we have to throw somebody out of one."

Half a dozen bearded freighters were lined up along the bar, a burly man in the middle apparently buying the drinks. At least he was dominating the conversation. He had a heavy voice that overrode the others, and Dave, glancing at him, suspected that he was a man who made a habit of overriding those around him in more ways than talk.

"I tell you them damned heathens have got to be run out of Colorado," the burly man was saying. "If Uncle Sam won't do it, then us that lives in Colorado has got to. The governor is sending all the guns he can get his hands on. What we ought to do is to take them guns and sashay over to the Uncompahgre and shoot every red bastard we can find from Chief Ouray on down to the papooses."

"Might be a few squaws we could use," one of the men said, and laughed as if it were a great joke.

"Who in hell wants a squaw?" the burly man demanded. "They stink like hell. Besides, they wouldn't know what to do if a man got one of 'em out in the brush."

The hotel man hurried back to listen to the freighters, opposite Dave and Kelso. He asked impatiently, "What'll you have, gents?"

"Whisky," Kelso said.

"The same," Dave said. "Who's the big man that's doing all the gabbing?"

"Duke Conway." The hotel man set two glasses and a bottle on the bar. "He sure knows what to do with the damned Injuns. Too bad he ain't governor instead of Pitkin."

The hotel man hurried back to listen to the freighters. Dave said, "You know this Conway, Kelso?"

"No." Kelso shook his head. "There's plenty out here that's the same stripe he is, but I never ran into this one before."

Kelso poured the drinks and set the bottle down. Dave's blood began to pound in his ears as he listened to Conway's violent talk. The freighter was expressing the general sentiment of the frontier, and, for that matter, the sentiment of the Colorado press and most of the state officials, but this didn't make it any easier for Dave to listen to it.

Here was the kind of talk that could infuriate men to the place where they would cross the reservation boundary with the idea of exterminating the Indians. If that happened, it would cause a blood bath that would make the Thornburgh battle on Milk Creek seem like a mere skirmish.

"It ain't right for a bunch of damned, lazy, no-good savages to sit on their butts and keep human beings like us from settling on that good land on the Gunnison and the Grand," Conway was saying. "By now they've killed Meeker. Chances are all the troops are dead, too. Same as Custer. So what happens? We sit here talking while them red devils around the Los Pinos Agency pick up their guns and clean out towns like Ouray and Gunnison. By God, I tell you we ought to wipe 'em out. If I ever get a chance to make a good Indian out of a live one, I'll do it. I ain't staying here with my wagon 'cause I'm scared of 'em, neither. I'm rolling out in the morning."

Dave had heard all he could stand. He picked up his glass and downed his drink, then he wheeled and stalked out of the barroom. Kelso caught up with him, asking, "What got into you? I'll buy you another . . ."

"No thanks," Dave said. "One's enough for me tonight."

He turned toward the stairs. Kelso grabbed his arm. "What made you sore? I was a little huffy there at the table, but hell, I got over it."

"It wasn't you," Dave said quickly. "I just couldn't listen to what that damn fool Conway was saying without knocking his head off. I'd have done it if I thought it would do any good."

Kelso's face showed his surprise. "I didn't hear him say anything to make you sore. A thousand men are saying the same thing. If Governor Pitkin is shipping guns like Conway says, the thing he's talking about could happen."

"I know, I know," Dave said hotly. "That's what makes me so mad. A man like that can provoke an Indian war if he keeps talking. What's already happened is bad enough, but if the Utes over there at Los Pinos start to fight, we'll have a lot of good people killed along with the sons of bitches like Conway. And I'll tell you something else, Kelso. All the fault is not on the side of the Utes. Well, I'd better go to bed before I lose my temper."

He climbed the stairs and strode along the hall to his room. He went in, closed the door and hung his corduroy coat over a chair, then sat down on the edge of the bed and pulled off his boots. He lay down and closed his eyes, the rage that was in him slowly dying.

He could not sleep. An old question that had plagued him from the time he was a boy came back into his mind. Were the dominant qualities and talents that were in a man born in him? If so, what was their source? Did they grow from seeds planted during some past life or during the period in which the human spirit is nurtured before it enters a human body? Or were they derived from the race consciousness which had evolved in mankind down through the ages? Or had the qualities and talents which made Dave Rand what he was today been developed by what had happened to him during his twenty-seven years of living?

He still did not have any answers that made sense. So, because he could not sleep, he lay staring at the dark ceiling and hearing the rumble of sound from the barroom, his thoughts going back to the years when he had grown up on Alonzo Freeman's ranch in the San Luis Valley.

3

When Dave Rand was a boy of seven, his folks moved to Denver. This was in '59. His mother made the living while his father hunted gold that he never found. When the Civil War broke out, his father joined the Union Army and was killed in Glorieta Pass. Later on Mrs. Rand married a stockman named Alonzo Freeman and she and Dave went to live on his ranch in the San Luis Valley.

Freeman was a lanky, weather-burned man in his fifties. He ran a herd of cattle and traded horses with the Utes, then sold the horses to the Army. He took a liking to Dave from the first and taught him about horses and cattle and how to use the tools that a cowboy used.

Freeman gave Dave a buckskin gelding, telling him it was his as long as he took care of the animal. Dave's father had been practically a stranger, so he had never loved him as a father, but he loved Alonzo Freeman from the minute the rancher led the horse out of the corral and gave him to Dave.

He was only ten, but he was big for his age, and did what was close to a man's work almost from the beginning. When he wasn't working, he was riding or hunting with a Ute boy named Arvado who was an orphan and had been raised by a neighbor family named Nelson as if he were their own child.

Arvado was two years older than Dave, but no taller, and like most Utes, he was stocky and very dark-skinned. He spoke English as well as his foster parents. The Utes often rode past the Freeman and Nelson ranches on their way to hunt buffalo, so he had a chance to practice his native tongue, as well.

Dave and Arvado often rode to Fort Garland to watch the soldiers drill or to visit with the Utes when they camped nearby. To Dave an Indian camp was like an active, exciting beehive. There was always movement and noise and the possibility of danger, although this was largely in his imagination, particularly after Kit Carson took command of the fort.

The biggest thrill of all came from watching a band of warriors gallop into camp. It seemed to Dave there were hundreds of them, their faces daubed with paint, the guns in their hands. Dave soon learned to recognize Ouray, a stocky chief in his middle thirties, and Shavano, the war chief. Both had great reputations as fighters against the Comanches, Kiowas, Arapahoes, and Cheyennes.

These were the happy days, days that Dave wished would go on and on, days of hunting and fishing and visiting and riding and doing the kind of work he loved. Then, suddenly, in the fall of 1867 his way of life was taken from him.

Alonzo Freeman had driven a horse herd to Fort Garland to sell, and Dave had gone deer hunting with Arvado. Winter was at hand, the first light snow having dusted the crest of Blanca Peak. On their way home they talked about their bad luck, Dave wondering how he could have missed the one good shot he'd had at a big buck that would have meant camp meat if he's brought him down. Then they talked about the horses Alonzo had sold and how much gold he had brought back from the fort.

"It'll be a pocketful," Arvado said. "Ain't many men as good at horse trading as 'Lonzo Freeman. Leastwise that's what Pap says."

"He's good, all right," Dave agreed, "but I wish he'd kept that bay. He was the fastest horse on the ranch, and I told 'Lonzo I could win a race against any horse the Utes had. We could have won every pony they had if . . ." They had reached the yard and suddenly he realized that Arvado wasn't listening. "What's wrong?"

The young Indian didn't answer for a time. He slipped out of his saddle and was moving around Dave in a wide circle, then he ran back to his horse and pulled his rifle from the scabbard.

"Something's wrong," Arvado said.

Dave knew from years of experience with the young Indian that he was not one to go off half-cocked or be unduly alarmed about unseen dangers. Dave stepped down and drew his rifle from the boot, asking, "How do you know?"

"I seen Alonzo's horse in the corral," Arvado said, "and then I seen some tracks of horses leaving like the riders was in a hurry, so I got down and took a good look. Two men ran out of the house. Two horses left fast. They was shod." He glanced at Dave, his dark eyes expressionless "White men don't hurry like that unless something's wrong. Maybe more in the house. I dunno."

For a moment Dave stared at Arvado, asking himself why anything should be wrong. Alonzo had just gone to Fort Garland, a trip he made every week or so. Then Dave whirled and ran into the house, remembering that Arvado had said they were white men.

He stopped just inside the front door, a sob breaking out of him. His mother lay in a pool of blood near the fireplace, her body and face turned ugly and grotesque by death. Alonzo was sprawled in a bigger puddle of blood near the kitchen door.

For a time Dave could not move. He had trouble even breathing. He felt as if the sky had dropped on him. The thought of living without his mother and Alonzo had never occurred to him before.

He made himself cross the room and feel for his mother's pulse. She was dead, and then he saw that she had been scalped. He moved to Alonzo and felt of his pulse. There wasn't any. He, too, had been scalped.

Dave turned and stumbled out of the house and into the late afternoon sunlight. Arvado looked at him questioningly. He said hoarsely, "They're dead, but it wasn't white men who killed them. It was Indians. They've been scalped."

"No," Arvado said. "I told you the horses were shod.

The men wore boots, not moccasins. They wanted you to think the Utes done it.''

He was probably right. Alonzo had never had trouble with the Utes. Then Dave knew. Alonzo had come back from the fort with a small fortune in gold. Somehow the murderers had found out and had killed him for it.

Dave turned to his horse and shoved his rifle back into the boot. He asked, ''Can we find them?''

''We'll find them,'' Arvado said. ''They're hurrying too fast. I followed their tracks a ways when you was in the house. They're headed for La Veta Pass.'' He shook his head. ''They won't make it before dark.''

Dave mounted and motioned for Arvado to go ahead. The young Ute was the best tracker Dave had ever seen. Even Alonzo had admitted that he was as good as a hound dog. Arvado did not ride fast, but watched the ground ahead of his horse and kept a steady pace. The fugitives were not trying to reach the road, but seemed to be picking the easiest route they could find through the scattered cedars.

Dave, glancing at his friend, thought that at times Arvado lost the trail, and then, guessing the route the killers would take, had picked it up again. The danger was that the light might fail too much for Arvado to follow the trail, or find it again if he lost it.

Arvado had guessed right when he'd said the two men would not reach the pass. He stopped just before they topped a steep ridge, dismounted, and motioned for Dave to do the same. For a moment Dave stared at him wondering if he had gone crazy.

Arvado whispered, ''We'll find them soon. One horse has gone lame.''

Dave understood then and stepped down. They tied their horses and, carrying their rifles, moved silently up the slope. Dave remembered there was a spring just beyond the crest. A moment later he smelled smoke and told himself Arvado was still guessing right. The fugitives had stopped and made camp.

Near the ridge top Arvado dropped flat, motioning for Dave to do the same. They wormed their way to the crest.

Lying on their bellies, they saw two soldiers who were squatting beside a fire not far below them. Dave judged they had not been here long because they had not unsaddled or started supper.

The soldiers were quarreling about something. Presently one of them raised his voice and shouted angrily, "By God, Harris, I knowed you was a fool. We didn't have to kill 'em. Now you've got a lame horse. Well, I ain't gonna let 'em hang me just because you're stupid. I'm taking my horse and riding out of . . ."

He didn't finish his sentence. The other soldier shot him through the belly without giving him the slightest warning. The killer stood there watching the other man die, then he shoved his revolver into the holster. He stooped and, picking up several buckskin bags, turned toward one of the horses.

Dave rose, his cocked rifle on the ready. "Drop 'em," he yelled. "Get your hands up."

The soldier cursed and dropped the bags and tried to draw his revolver. Dave shot him before he had it clear of leather. Dave saw the man spin half-around and drop, and then he ran down the slope, Arvado remaining on the ridge top, his rifle lined on the soldier Dave had shot. But the man was dead. When Dave motioned to Arvado, he rose and trotted downslope.

For a moment the two boys looked at each other, a bond of understanding between them that Dave had never known with anyone else except his mother and Alonzo Freeman. Without a word they picked up the buckskin bags and loaded the dead men on their horses and returned to the ranch. Dave didn't know what to do then, so Arvado said, "Let's go get Pap."

Clyde Nelson listened when they told him what had happened, then he said, "Them bastards must have seen 'Lonzo get the gold at the fort. Chances are they was figuring on deserting anyway. After Alonzo was killed, they must have killed your ma to keep her from identifying them."

They buried Dave's mother and Alonzo on the slope of Blanca Peak above the house. Dave stayed with the Nelsons that winter, but nothing was the same. He wasn't sure what he wanted to do. He often thought of what his mother had said to him once after they'd heard his father had been killed: "You were born into a cruel world, David, and there are times when you have to be tough to journey through it, but be sure of one thing. Be proud of your journey. Don't live in a way that will make you ashamed of it later."

He knew now the world was far more cruel than he had thought, so cruel that it was hard to keep from hating everything and everyone. When he said anything like that to Clyde Nelson, he was instantly reproved.

"The best way to destroy yourself is to start hating everybody," Nelson said. "What you need to do is to get out of here and go to school. 'Lonzo didn't have any kin, so his outfit belongs to you. Sell out and go to school somewhere. You'll have plenty of money. Use it to make something out of yourself."

When spring came he knew Nelson was right. He wasn't sure he could stand the discipline of school, but he knew he had to leave the valley. So he sold out, shook hands with the Nelsons and Arvado and rode away. He never saw Arvado again.

4

The stage, with Sharon Morgan, Dave, and Kelso the only passengers, wheeled out of Cleora before sunup, crossed the river soon after it left the hotel, and then rolled west along the fork known as the South Arkansas. The road held to the higher ground to avoid the swamp lowland that was covered by one great beaver pond after another.

"You're either a brave or a foolish woman to go on," Dave told Sharon. "I guess nobody else except us is willing to risk his life."

She smiled. "I'd say the same applies to you about being brave or foolish," she said. "I'll admit to being foolish. I'm as scared of the Indians as I was yesterday, and I know the farther I go the more likely we are to run into them." She shrugged, and added, "But I might as well go on. I don't want to stay another night in that terrible hotel."

"It'll be worse in Gunnison," Kelso said. "You may not even find a hotel."

"Then I'll sleep on the ground," she said. "It couldn't be any worse."

A moment later they whipped past a plodding freight outfit. Kelso, recognizing Duke Conway, said, "We almost had some excitement in the bar last night. Rand here didn't like the talk that freighter was making. He said if he hadn't walked out he'd have knocked the man's head off."

Sharon, riding beside Dave, gave him a questioning glance. "What did he say that made you so mad?"

Irritated, Dave was silent a moment. He did not want to try to explain his feeling about the Indian trouble because it was not entirely a matter of logic. He said sourly, "You've got a long tongue, Kelso."

"Why, you've got no cause to complain about the length of my tongue," Kelso said innocently. "It's just that I thought it was kind o' funny the way you got hot under the collar because Conway was saying what everybody else in Colorado is saying."

"Now you've aroused my curiosity," Sharon said. "What happened?"

Dave started to say it wasn't important, but Kelso wouldn't let it lie. He said, "Rand got sore because the freighter was talking about running the Utes out of Colorado. As far as I'm concerned, the freighter was right. The Utes have got to go."

Sharon's blue eyes were normally filled with good humor, her full-lipped mouth sweetly shaped, but now her cheeks turned red and her lips thinned as she drew them down at the corners. Her scornful eyes were fixed on Dave's face, but several seconds passed before she had her temper controlled enough to speak.

"I don't like to quarrel with anyone," she said slowly, "especially with a man who has been as kind as you have, Mr. Rand, but why in Heaven's name shouldn't the Utes be run out of Colorado?"

Dave felt as if he had been slapped in the face. He moistened his lips, thinking about his answer before he gave it, then he said, speaking as slowly as Sharon had, "Because the Utes have a treaty giving them the land they're living on. We've already talked them out of the San Juan because we've found out it's good mining country. That's the story of our treatment of the Indians clear back to the beginning of our history. We give them land and promise it's to be theirs forever, then when our settlers want it or when gold is discovered like it was in the Black Hills, we tear up the treaty and tell them to sign a new one."

Sharon turned her head to look out of the window on her side of the coach, her cheeks still red, her lips pressed tightly together. She was willing to let it drop, Dave thought, but Kelso was bound to keep the pot boiling. He asked, "What was that you said about all the fault not being on one side?"

Sharon's head snapped around, her eyes filled with indignation. She said hotly, "That seems to me a fool thing to say. Who was it that killed Thornburgh and some of his men, maybe all of them by now? And who was it that killed Meeker and his people, if they are killed like most people think?"

Dave took a long breath, holding his silence while he fought an impulse to kick Kelso on the shin. He said, "We don't know the whole story about what provoked the White River Utes. It wouldn't be in the newspapers because to my knowledge there isn't a journalist in the state of Colorado who has the courage to give the Indians' side of the trouble."

"I doubt that they have a side," Sharon said angrily. "They're like vicious children who have not been disciplined."

"In many ways they are like children," Dave agreed, "but even vicious children do not explode into violence the way the White River Utes have unless there's a cause for it." He turned to Kelso. "It seems to me you missed the point last night."

"No, I didn't," Kelso said smugly. "You said definitely . . ."

"Now wait a minute," Dave said in exasperation. "The point that riled me was Conway saying they ought to take the guns that Governor Pitkin is sending to the frontier towns and go onto the reservation and wipe out the Uncompahgre Utes. They aren't the ones who have gone on a rampage. It would be criminal to attack . . ."

"Criminal!" Sharon shouted the word above the clatter of the fast-moving coach. "But you condone anything the Utes do as if it wasn't criminal."

"Not at all," he said quickly. "The White River Utes should be punished. What I said was that we don't know, you and me and all the John and Jane Does who read the newspapers, what caused the outbreak."

"I'd like to know what kind of a white man you are," she said scornfully.

"I'm one white man," he said, "who believes that the word of our government is as sacred as an individual's and should be kept. Furthermore, I do not believe that all the Utes in Colorado should be punished for what one bunch of them did. Ouray is the chief at the Los Pinos Agency and he always has been friendly to the whites. I say it is criminal to break our treaty and run the Utes off their home land simply because a lot of land-hungry boomers want it."

Sharon's hands were tightly clenched on her lap, her gaze on Kelso's face as if seeking his agreement. "I think all Indians are alike whether they live on White River or the Uncompahgre. They're savages. They're dirty and greasy and they smell bad. I see no reason why they should be allowed to keep all of this land and let it go to waste the way it is. What do you think, Mr. Kelso?"

"I agree with you," Kelso said amiably. "Twelve million acres I think it is they've got. They don't farm it. They don't even raise cows or sheep to amount to anything, so it sure don't add nothing to the wealth of the state." He grinned, and added, "As for me, I'd like to have a quarter section of it."

Sharon turned her head to look at Dave. "You are the only white man in Colorado who would talk this way. If you stay here, you will find that out."

"They'll lynch him if they hear that kind of talk in Gunnison," Kelso said.

Dave turned his head to stare at the sagebrush-covered valley to the north. He had not asked for this argument; he would have avoided it if he could. He knew he could not change Sharon's attitude with words any more than he could have changed Duke Conway's if he had argued with the freighter last night. Opinions and attitudes stem from people's emotions, not their reason, and after what had happened on Milk Creek and what had probably happened at the agency, the emotions of all Colorado people would sweep away their sense of logic.

He slowly swung back to look at Sharon. He said, "It's a funny thing how differently people in the East feel about the Indians. Before the war men like William Lloyd Garrison and Wendell Phillips fought to free the slaves. Now that the slaves have been freed, these men are fighting for the Indians.''

''Then they'd better come West to where the Indians are,'' Sharon said hotly. ''They stay back there in Boston and write their articles and preach their sermons and they never even smell an Indian or have a relative murdered by one.'' She moistened her lips with the tip of her tongue. ''Maybe you should have stayed with the rest of the Eastern do-gooders.''

He shook his head. ''I have a job to do here and I'll do it if I live long enough. There is another thing, Miss Morgan. Jesus taught that we reap what we sow. I guess that's something Christians don't like to think about, but I'm convinced that nations reap what they sow just the same as individuals do.''

Kelso laughed. ''Oh, come on, Rand. You're talking pretty highfalutin. I'm thinking about right now, 1879, not 1899 or even 1889. I want some of that good Ute land just like a lot of other people do. You ain't gonna turn a whole river around so it will run the other way. If you don't know which direction this river's running, I can tell you mighty quick.''

''So can I,'' Sharon said. ''I'd like to know, Mr. Rand, if you have ever actually seen a single live Ute Indian? You're an Eastern man, so you're talking theory just like all the others.''

''No,'' Dave said. ''I'm not an Eastern man. I lived here in Colorado until I went East a few years ago. Yes, I've seen quite a few Indians. When I was a boy in the San Luis Valley, my best friend was a Ute about my age.''

She was silent then, plainly surprised by what he had said. They reached Poncha Springs, crossed the South Arkansas, and started climbing, the canyon walls closing in on both sides. Later, when they reached the first relay station and had had a chance to stretch, Dave shouldered Kelso away from the coach so Sharon could not hear their talk.

''What are you trying to do?'' Dave demanded. ''I

wasn't looking for a quarrel. I ought to knock your damned head off.''

"But you got a quarrel, didn't you?" Kelso laughed softly. "I'll tell you something, my Indian-loving friend. I promised you a run for your money. You made me look like an ignoramus last night at the table, so I figured I owed you a little trouble. Getting you started talking about the Utes seemed the proper way to do it.''

"I still ought to knock your head off," Dave said. "I didn't intend to make you look like an ignoramus, but you intended to make me look bad in front of Sharon on the Indian business.''

"That I did," Kelso agreed. "That I did.''

Fresh horses had been hooked up and Dave and Kelso hurried back to the coach. Dave pulled the door shut and glanced at Kelso who was looking out of the window as smugly as ever.

"I should tell you why I feel the way I do, Mr. Rand," Sharon said in an apologetic voice as if regretting her outburst. "It's not that I want any of the Ute land, but I have reason to hate them. To be afraid to them, too. You see, I was very small when we first moved to Colorado. The Utes often came to our house and begged for something to eat and my mother gave it to them if she had any. She was afraid not to. I was terrified whenever they stopped. I remember one time they were coming back from a fight with the Arapahoes and they had some fresh scalps. I was physically sick after they left, and for years I dreamed about seeing those scalps. I guess I had nightmares because I'd wake up at night screaming.''

"I can see why you'd be afraid of them," Dave said, "but I don't see why you should hate them.''

"That's something else. I'm not done. I don't like to talk about it or even think about it, but as long as I started, I'll tell you the rest." She stared at her hands which were folded on her lap, silent for a moment, then she went on, "My uncle was murdered by the Utes last summer. He was more than an uncle, almost a brother to me. He was on his ranch in Middle Park and he hadn't done a thing to hurt the Indians. Maybe they were drunk. I don't know, but I do know they rode past his place and shot him.''

She raised her head to look at him. She said in a low tone, ''They were the same White River Utes who by now have probably murdered Nathan Meeker and his people at the agency when all Meeker was trying to do was to help them.''

''I'm sorry about your uncle,'' Dave said. ''My mother and stepfather were murdered by white men.''

''Oh, I didn't know.'' She hesitated, then added, ''But you don't hate all white men. Is that what you're getting at?''

''That's right,'' he said. ''I don't.''

She lowered her head again to stare at her hands. Presently she said, ''I wish I could feel that way about the Utes. I truly do.''

They were silent then. Dave glanced at the pines struggling for life in the rocks of the canyon wall. He understood why she felt as she did. At least she had reason to hate the Utes and therefore was different from most people who, like Vince Kelso, simply wanted their land. Then he wondered how he would feel if his parents had been murdered by Indians instead of white men.

The stage rolled into Gunnison with the dusk light so thin that Dave could not make out much of the town as he stepped from the coach and turned to give Sharon a hand. The day had been long, the trip tiring, and still the girl appeared almost as fresh as she had that morning.

''You look as if you could go another twelve hours,'' Dave told her.

She smiled and shook her head. ''It's because the light is bad. Now I'm wondering if I'll find a place to sleep tonight.''

Kelso climbed to the boot and found her bag. ''We'll get a room for you,'' he said as he tossed the bag to Dave.

Still, it turned out to be a problem. Gunnison was too new to have even a hotel as good as the one in Cleora that Sharon had called ''terrible.'' The town had the appearance of a boom camp, being made up largely of tents and hastily built log cabins. After an hour of searching, Dave and Kelso finally found a place for Sharon to stay. It was in a boardinghouse run by a woman named Mrs. Pattison. She ordinarily did not keep overnight guests, but she agreed to fix a cot in her kitchen.

"We don't get many good women in this place, though we get plenty of the other kind." Mrs. Pattison glared at them as if expecting them to defend the "other kind," but when both men remained silent, she added, "It'd be a shame not to treat a good woman right when she does come. It'll be five dollars."

"Thank you," Dave said. "We'll go get her." As they walked back to the hotel where they had left Sharon in the lobby, he said, "The good Lord protect us from righteous women."

"Yeah, and it would have been a shame for her to have missed the five dollars," Kelso said, "but it looks like Sharon's lucky at that, beds being as scarce as they are."

The best that Dave and Kelso could do for supper was a greasy meal in a tent restaurant. When they finished, the restaurant man shoved several sheets of paper under their noses and said, "If you gents are staying in Gunnison, you're going to have to do your part. Sign up."

"What the hell?" Kelso demanded belligerently. "We ain't staying and we ain't signing up for nothing."

Kelso would have handed the papers back, but Dave took them from him, his eyes scanning the writing. At the top in a neat hand were the words: *Resolutions of the citizens of Gunnison City to consider methods of defense against possible attacks of Indians. We, the undersigned citizens of Gunnison do hereby pledge ourselves to answer any call to arms necessary to defense against an Indian attack.*

Below were the signatures of about fifty men, some with the words *"no arms"* written after their names, and others with *"Remington rifle"* or *"double-barreled shotgun"* or similar information. One man even had *shotgun, rifles, and three revolvers."*

Turning to the last page Dave read:

All persons having more arms than necessary for their own use will leave them at the post office subject to the distribution of Captain Jennings.

Signal. *One shot by a scout shall be answered by two shots by party in charge of arsenal.*

Resolved, *That Captain Jennings detail a sufficient number of men to dig rifle-pits in the places directed by a committee of 5: these pits to be sufficiently near for each to sustain the other.*

Resolved, *That Col. Hall, Capt. Mullen, W. Harland, Judge Smith and Mr. Woodward shall address a petition to Gov. Pitkin asking for sufficient arms and ammunition and if necessary, men to defend or assist in defending the town.*

Dave handed the papers back to the restaurant man. "Do you actually expect an Indian attack? Or is this some kind of a joke?"

"It ain't no joke," the restaurant man shot back. "We're right smack up against the reservation line and we'd be the first to get it if that goddamned bunch of red devils over there on the Uncompahgre decide to lift some hair. We figure to be ready."

"Come on," Dave said to Kelso as he turned to the door.

"Ain't you gonna sign?" the restaurant man yelled. "Don't expect us to protect you if you ain't willing to protect yourself."

Dave swung around, fighting an impulse to tell the man what he thought of this kind of panic, but there was no point in it. Kelso had not been far wrong when he'd said that morning that Dave would hang if the Gunnison men heard what he'd said in the stage.

"You heard what my friend said," Dave told him. "We're going out tomorrow on the stage."

Dave and Kelso walked out of the tent, leaving the man sputtering about them being damned fools to risk their necks that way. As they walked back to the hotel, Kelso said, "I guess you've got business on the reservation, so maybe you've got to go, but me'n Sharon don't. Sometimes I wonder if we're as crazy as people say we are."

"Then stay here," Dave said.

Kelso laughed shortly. "I won't admit I'm as scared as these people, so I guess I'll go on. Panic is kind o' catching, though. 'Bout like measles."

When they reached the hotel, they found there was only one bed left in the big, barnlike room behind the cubicle that served as a lobby. The beds were set so close together that they nearly touched. Some were occupied, some were empty but were occupied later in the night. Men were coming and going constantly. Apparently some had been on guard duty and others were leaving to relieve men who were still out there in the darkness. Dave wondered if a number of them were digging rifle pits.

Kelso went to sleep at once, but the constant moving of the men kept Dave awake. He doubted that anyone except Kelso slept. The ones who were in bed carried on conversations in hushed tones as if they were at a funeral. He finally dropped off, but woke with the first opalescent light of dawn. He shook Kelso awake and pulled on his boots and slipped outside, Kelso yawning as he followed Dave into the street.

Sleepy-eyed men who were returning from guard duty drifted along the street, rifles or shotguns in their hands. When Dave and Kelso reached Mrs. Pattison's boardinghouse, they sat down to breakfast with Sharon and soon learned that she had been exposed to more panic talk.

"Mrs. Pattison swears we'll be scalped the instant we cross the reservation line," Sharon whispered.

"Did she scare you into staying in Gunnison?" Dave asked in a low tone.

Sharon smiled and shook her head. "The beds have been getting worse each night. They just have to be better somewhere west of here."

"I've heard that the beds and grub are good at Major Leslie's," Kelso said.

"You'd better stay here and rest up a few days," Dave said.

"No." Sharon shook her head. "I'm sleepy and tired and I'm still scared, but I started for Ouray and that's where I'm going."

"I'll have to stay if Major Leslie isn't home," Dave said. "I've got to interview him."

Leslie was a well-known personality on the frontier, a man who had distinguished himself as a cavalry officer during the Civil War, and then, coming West, he had continued to distinguish himself. With several other prospectors, he had made the first strike near the mining camp of Ouray, he had helped found the town, and then, being a friend to the Utes, he had been given permission to operate a ranch inside the reservation. He had settled on the Cimarron, had put up buildings, and for the past year or more had run an overnight stop on the road between Gunnison and the Los Pinos Agency and the mining camp of Ouray which lay south of the agency.

Dave was looking forward to meeting him, for he had the reputation of understanding the Utes better than anyone else in Colorado. If there was any danger of an outbreak along the Uncompahgre, Leslie would have known it and have warned the border towns. The fact that no such warning had come was to Dave the surest sign that Chief Ouray still controlled his people.

The stage left on time, the few bystanders prophesying that neither the driver nor the passengers would be alive to reach Leslie's place, that all four of them must be tired of living and were determined to commit suicide. Mrs. Pattison stood on the plank walk, waving her handkerchief and crying.

When the town was behind them, Sharon said, "Mrs. Pattison told me it was a pity that my beautiful blond hair would hang in the lodge of some stinking Ute buck."

"It would be a pity," Dave agreed. "So much of a pity that it won't happen."

Sharon sighed and closed her eyes. "No, I'm sure it won't," she said. A moment later she was asleep, her head on Dave's shoulder.

"You're the luckiest man I ever seen," Kelso said softly. "How about changing places with me at the next relay station?"

"Nothing doing," Dave said. "You got your whacks at

me when you worked up that argument yesterday morning. Now you can take your medicine.''

She must not have got her five dollars' worth out of Mrs. Pattison's cot,'' Kelso said, ''or else she just likes the shoulder you're offering her.''

''Mrs. Pattison scared her so much she probably couldn't sleep,'' Dave said, yawning. ''I didn't get my money's worth, either.''

They were silent then, and presently Dave dropped off to sleep, too. For miles the road followed the Gunnison River, crossing occasionally when the terrain demanded it, then swung south. Later in the day the stage crossed the turbulent Lake Fork of the Gunnison on a narrow bridge, then toiled up the switchbacks to Blue Mesa and wheeled down the western slope to the Cimarron. The shadow of the coach was a long, grotesque shape on the ground when they rolled into the Leslie yard and men ran to them to take the horses.

The major was not there, Dave learned. He had gone to the Los Pinos Agency and there was no telling where he was now, with conditions the way they were. Dave decided to wait rather than to go on and hope to find him.

''He's never gone more'n a few days,'' one of the men said. ''He'll be back afore long.''

The beds were comfortable, the food excellent for a stage stop, and the next morning Sharon came downstairs to breakfast looking refreshed and rested. After they had eaten, Dave walked with her to the coach. The gray traveling suit she had been wearing during the days when they were in the stage was wrinkled and dirty, and she apologized for it.

''Never apologize,'' he said, smiling. ''Your enemies won't believe you and your friends don't need it.''

Kelso caught up with them in time to hear Dave's remark. He grimaced as he said, ''It seems that we still have the philosopher with us.''

Dave told himself he could hate Vince Kelso if he worked at it, but he ignored him as he said, ''I'm your friend, Sharon, and don't you forget it after you get to Ouray and I'm not around to remind you of it.''

"I won't," she promised

She stood beside the coach, looking at Dave as if wanting to impress a picture of him on her mind.

"I can't begin to thank you for the kindness you and Vince have shown me from the moment the train pulled into Canon City," she said. "I'm sorry about our argument, and we certainly didn't change each other's opinion."

"We didn't for a fact," he agreed.

As if giving way to a sudden impulse, she leaned forward and kissed him on the cheek, then turned quickly and stepped into the coach. Kelso, his mouth close to Dave's ear, said, "You're still a lucky man."

"You're the lucky one," Dave said. "You'll have her to yourself now."

"And I aim to make hay while the sun shines," Kelso said. "I'll see she forgets she ever met you."

Kelso stepped into the stage and sat down beside Sharon. As the coach wheeled away, he made a derisive gesture as if to say that today she would sleep on his shoulder. Dave stood there in the chill morning air watching the stage until it disappeared downstream.

Fate had brought the three of them together, then had parted them. Dave wondered if they would ever be together again. But whether they were or not, he would see Sharon, he told himself. No matter what happened, he would see her again.

5

Dave had to wait several days for Major Leslie, longer than he expected and longer than he wanted to wait, but he was afraid to take the stage to the agency. He had no idea whether his man was there or not, so he might miss him, and he considered it imperative that he talk to him before he went on.

Dave was sitting on the front porch smoking late one afternoon when a man rode in from the west. Dismounting at one of the corrals, he turned his horse over to a hostler who stepped out of the log barn. Dave threw his cigar away and rose, watching the man who was tall and stood very straight as if he had never forgotten his training as a soldier.

It was Leslie, Dave guessed, and stepped off the porch and strode toward him. "I'm Dave Rand," he said when he reached the man. "Are you Major Leslie?"

"I'm Sam Leslie." He frowned, and repeated the word "Rand" as if he thought he should be able to place it and could not.

"I have a letter from Carl Schurz, the Secretary of the Interior," Dave said. "I've been waiting to see you. The letter will tell you why."

Leslie took the envelope, removed the single sheet of paper, and unfolded it. He read the letter, then looked over it at Dave as if making a careful appraisal of him. He was in his early forties, Dave judged, dark complexioned with a week's growth of stubble on his face, eyes that were close to being black, and a bristly brown mustache.

"He says you're a Special Agent of the Department of

the Interior," Leslie said slowly. "I don't savvy. Why
did Schurz send you to me?"

"Because General Adams said you knew more about the
Utes than any man in Colorado," Dave said, "and about
the Los Pinos Agency in particular. If he hadn't told me
that, I would have gone to the White River Agency first
because we knew that was where trouble was most likely
to come, so in a way I owe you my life. I suppose I would
have been dead if I had gone there."

"You suppose right," Leslie said. "Just before I left
the Los Pinos Agency, the word came that Colonel Merritt
had arrived at the battle field and found most of the
soldiers alive. The fighting is over for the time being,
mostly due to Ouray who ordered the Utes to quit. Merritt
went on to the agency and found that Meeker and every
white man there had been murdered."

"What about the women?"

"Apparently they are prisoners," Leslie answered. "At
least their bodies were not found, and Mrs. Price's children weren't, either. A runner who showed up at Ouray's
house said the three women and two children were being
held prisoners, but they may have been murdered by this
time."

Dave took a long breath. He was glad to be alive. No
one knew how close he had come to going to Rawlins
from Denver on the train instead of Canon City, and
traveling south from there to the White River Agency.

Thinking back to the decision he had made, he wondered if fate had preserved him for some future use. He
had actually made up his mind to go to White River before
he came here, and if he had not had a few minutes alone
with General Charles Adams who had once been the Los
Pinos agent, he would have gone to White River, and he
would certainly have been there at the time of the massacre.

"I hope you can give me some time," Dave said. "I'm
late now in getting off a report to the Secretary about the
Los Pinos Agency, and I want to talk to you before I write
it up. Oh, there is one thing. We thought it would be better
if I did not tell my real reason for being here. Ostensibly
I'm a reporter for a Washington newspaper."

"I understand." Leslie scratched his belly, grimacing. "I'm lousy. I've been with the Indians the last few days, so if Mrs. Patrick has some hot water, I'll have a bath and shave and I'll change my clothes. We'll talk afterward." He started toward the house, then swung back. "The stage had been coming through every day?"

Dave nodded. "Running empty most of the time, though. People are panicky and seem to think we'll have a war all along the frontier."

"Damn fools," Leslie said irritably. "Sometimes I think the whites actually want a war. It would be a sure way of moving the Utes out of Colorado."

He swung on his heel and strode into the house. Dave reached into his coat pocket for a cigar, his eyes on the man's ramrod back until he disappeared through the front door. He was a good man, Dave thought, as good a man as General Adams had said.

The stage came in presently, running empty as it had been every day since Dave had been here. When Dave asked the driver if people were getting over their panic, he said, "I think they'll be traveling in a day or two, now that the fighting's stopped and nothing's happened on the Uncompahgre. Folks are proddy as hell after hearing about Meeker. They want to hang every Ute in Colorado."

"Maybe it'd be just as well if they didn't travel for a while," Dave said.

The driver nodded. "The way some of the damn fools are talking, you'd think they was gonna ride onto the reservation and wipe out the whole Ute nation."

Mrs. Patrick rang the supper gong and Dave and the driver went into the house. A moment later Leslie came into the dining room, freshly shaven and smelling of bay rum. He spoke to the stage driver and sat down and began to eat ravenously. Dave and the driver sat down and ate. No one talked for several minutes until Leslie finished eating and leaned back and lighted a cigar.

"Just like a hog at a trough," he said, "but I haven't had a decent meal since I left here. All I need to do to appreciate Mrs. Patrick's cooking is to be gone for a while."

Leslie took the cigar out of his mouth and stared at it. "Funny thing, Rand. Some people are jealous of me because I talked Ouray and the other chiefs into letting me locate here. I told them that somebody would have to put in a road house, and it had better be me than a man they didn't know, so I got a choice location.

"Well, a lot of folks think I'm getting rich, but what they don't know is that the Utes like Mrs. Patrick's cooking, too. A whole band of them will stop here sometimes and she has to feed them. That damned Colorow was the worst. He's as big as a mountain, and he'll steal the hat right off your head if you don't look out."

Mrs. Patrick had come in with the coffeepot in time to hear what Leslie had said. "But I cured him, Major," she said. "One time he complained of being sick, so I gave him a big dose of Epsom salts. When he left he looked like a balloon with the air gone. He never came back."

The men laughed, and Dave asked, "Why do you have to feed them?"

"I don't have to, but I want to keep this place," Leslie said. "We all know that right or wrong, sooner or later the reservation will be thrown open to settlement. I think your Dutch Secretary wants to do right with the Indians, and so do the Eastern humanitarians, but the political pressure is too great. Senator Teller. Governor Pitkin. The Denver newspapers. Hell, they keep hollering 'The Utes must go.' I suppose this Meeker business will give them all the ammunition they need. Well, if I don't feed the Utes when they come by, they can run me off the place because I'm here by their permission. If I'm not here when the reservation is open, I won't get this property, so I've got to stay. Meanwhile the Utes are eating me out of house and home."

"I don't think Ouray will let them run you off," Dave said.

"Ouray's a sick man," Leslie said. "He's got Bright's disease. I doubt that he's alive next year at this time." He rose. "Now we can talk all you want, Rand. Let's get out of the dining room so Mrs. Patrick can clean up."

Leslie led Dave to his office in the back of the house, a small room cluttered with bridles and spurs and bits of leather and tally books the way most ranchers' offices were cluttered. Dave remembered that Alonzo Freeman had had a room much like this, the one room in the house that Dave's mother never dared clean.

"Sit down if you can find a place," Leslie said as he took a chair at his desk. "Tell me something. I've never met Secretary Schurz. He gets a cussing from the Grant Republicans and most of the Colorado politicians because he doesn't jump to their tune about the Utes, but I've kind of admired him for sticking to his guns."

"He's a good man," Dave said. "A darned good man. He grew up in Germany, you know, and barely got out with his life when the revolution of 1848 failed. He came to America, learned the English language and became an orator and a good writer. He served as a major general in the Civil War-Bull Run, Gettysburg, Chancellorsville—and afterward he was a Senator from Missouri. President Hayes thinks highly of him. Schurz is an honest man for one thing, which is something you don't always find in politicians."

Leslie laughed shortly. "You're right about that. But it seems to me he's wrong on this notion he's got about settling each Indian on a quarter section of land and opening the rest of the reservation to white settlement. Indians won't farm. The Utes won't anyhow. Take here at the Los Pinos Agency. Ouray has a farm, and he can get some of them to work for him, but they won't work for themselves and they won't work for white men."

"Wasn't that part of the trouble at White River?"

Leslie snorted in disgust. "Sure it was. Nathan Meeker brought on his own death. I was up there not long ago and the writing on the wall was plain enough to read for anyone who had eyes. I can't imagine a worse appointment for Indian agent than Meeker. He was a good man, so good that the goodness just poured out of him. He was bound to make farmers out of his Indians. Plowed up their horse pasture and told them to sell their ponies and that sort of foolishness that made them mad.

"It went from bad to worse, then he seemed to get kind of petulant, I guess, you'd say. He threatened them by telling them he'd bind them in chains and send them to Indian Territory. He set off the explosion when he sent for the troops. They thought he really was going to put them in chains and send them to Indian Territory.''

Leslie leaned forward, his cigar tucked into one corner of his mouth. "They hated him, Rand. God, how they hated him. Jack and some others even went to Denver and asked Governor Pitkin to get rid of Meeker. They sent word to Ouray to do all he could. Your Secretary should have transferred him before it was too late.''

"Schurz has a hundred other jobs besides running the Indian Bureau," Dave said. "That's why I'm here. He came West to investigate some of the agencies. There were several correspondents with him along with the President's son, Webb Hayes, and a few others. He had gone on west of Colorado when he heard that trouble was coming on White River, so he returned to Denver. He talked with several men including General Adams who wanted him to do something at once, but he didn't get around to it. That was how I got this appointment. He wanted a firsthand report on both the White River and Los Pinos Agencies, but he's hearing enough about White River without me going up there. After I get done in Colorado, I'll go south into Arizona and New Mexico. I'll probably work all winter.''

"Well, it would have saved trouble if he'd transferred Meeker," Leslie said. "To show you how much they hated Meeker, they put a logging chain around his neck and drove a stake through his mouth into the ground. That's the way they are. When they finally get worked up to the place where they go berserk, they go back about two generations.''

"Would the Uncompahgres do the same?''

"Not as long as Ouray is alive," Leslie answered. "After he dies I don't know. I suppose they might if they aren't handled right. The agent we have now is worse than nothing. We can stand a change here, too.''

Leslie rose and paced around the room, then he wheeled to face Dave. "Ouray understands what's happening. He's bought time for his people, though most of them don't savvy that and cuss him for not fighting. Now he's hoping to save at least the area where the agency is and maybe Grand Mesa. Between you and me, Rand, he'll be lucky to keep that much the way the pressure is piling up."

He leaned on his desk, his face mirroring his bitterness. "The stage brought in some of the Denver newspapers. One of them quoted General Pope as saying the Utes must go, that it's useless to try to prevent the whites from occupying mineral land and there's no reason to permit the Indians to occupy land like that. The law doesn't mean a damned thing, I guess, and if the newspapers can get somebody like John Pope to say this stuff, they make all they can out of it.

"Then Fred Pitkin says that the whites understand they are liable to be attacked in any part of the state at any time where the Indians are in sufficient force, and that unless the Indians are removed by the government, they must necessarily be exterminated."

Leslie slammed his fist down on the desk. "This is damned irresponsible talk for a governor to make. Of course it's possible the newspaper misquoted him. They'll do that just to whip up more sentiment against the Indians."

Leslie sat down at his desk and wiped a hand across his face. "I get so goddamned mad when I think of the lies that are put out just so people will get worked up enough to force the government to break its word with the Utes. Or all Indians, as far as that goes. One of the papers printed a rumor that Thornburgh's command had been killed to the man, that the Northern Utes had formed an alliance with the Arapahoes and a large number of the Arapahoes were with the Utes on the warpath. Well, I want to see the day when the Arapahoes throw in with the Utes."

Dave nodded, understanding what Leslie meant. The Utes and Arapahoes had been bitter enemies for years, and the chance that they would form even a temporary alliance against the whites seemed unbelievable.

Leslie took the cigar out of his mouth, his gaze on Dave's face. He said slowly, "There's one thing I haven't told you that you'll want to know. As long as there is the slightest chance the Meeker women and the Price children are alive, we've got to do what we can to rescue them. We wired Schurz what we had heard and he's asking General Adams to go onto the reservation and get them released if he can. I expect him on the stage tomorrow.''

"He'll get them if anyone can," Dave said. "Are you going with him?"

"That depends on what he wants," Leslie answered, "but I expect to. It seems to me we'd better outfit here and ride to Ouray's farm. He'll give us some guides and we'll strike out from there."

"What about Colonel Merritt?" Dave asked. "You would know more about these things than I do, but it seems to me the Indians will be hard to deal with if the soldiers are putting the squeeze on them."

"That's right," Leslie said. "It's the old scrap between the War Department and yours. If the War Department had its way, the Indians would be exterminated like Pitkin suggests and that would end the problem."

"I'd like to go with you and General Adams," Dave said. "You think there's any chance I could?"

"That also depends on him, but I think he might let you go." Leslie leaned forward. "You understand the risks? If the Meeker women have been murdered, we'll never get back to the agency. The Indians know they might get off pretty light with what's happened so far, but if they've killed the women, there'll be hell to pay. They're not fools. They'll know they might just as well add a few more scalps to what they've got."

"I understand that and I still want to go. Well, I'd better get upstairs and write my report. The Secretary will want to know what you've told me."

"Wait a minute," Leslie said. "When I first heard your name, it sounded familiar. Have you been West before?"

"I don't claim to be an Eastern man," Dave said. "I was in Denver when I was a boy, then I lived in San Luis Valley until my mother and stepfather were murdered. I went to school in Denver as long as I could stand it, then I worked for the *Daily News* awhile. I finally gravitated back to Washington. I guess I worked for a dozen newspapers between here and there.''

Leslie seemed lost in thought so completely that Dave wondered if he had heard a word he'd said. Suddenly the major snapped his fingers. "Now I remember. You ever know a man named Clyde Nelson?''

"Sure. Clyde and his wife were our closest neighbors in the San Luis Valley. They raised a Ute boy named Arvado. He was my best friend.''

"Nelson is working at the agency," Leslie said. "He'll want to see you. His wife died several years ago, so he sold out and left the valley. He's been helping with the agency herd for a couple of years.''

"Isn't Arvado with him?''

Leslie hesitated, then he said grimly, "Arvado was murdered by a white man named Rich. That seems the reason Clyde's wife died. Shock, I suppose. Clyde couldn't stand living there alone, so he started drifting after he sold his ranch.''

For a moment Dave couldn't move. He had trouble breathing. He had taken it for granted that he would see Arvado while he was in Colorado, but he had not realized until that moment how much he had counted on it. He asked finally, "How did it happen?''

"Rich was drunk. He'd lost his wife and children to the Comanches and I suppose he was kind of crazy. Anyhow, he was at Fort Garland when Arvado rode into the fort to see about selling some cattle. This bastard saw him and pulled his gun and cut loose without saying a word.''

"Did they hang him?''

Leslie laughed shortly. "Did you ever hear of a white man hanging because he killed an Indian?''

"Where is he?" Dave demanded. "By God, I'll take care of him . . .''

"No need to," Leslie said. "Rich was found dead on the road between Fort Garland and Alamosa. It was just a couple of days after he killed Arvado. They never found out who did it. He'd been shot in the guts, so he must have died slow and hard.''

"Clyde?''

"Who knows?" Leslie shrugged. "It's a good guess, all right, but he never said."

Dave turned and walked along the hall to the front of the house. He climbed the stairs to his room, lighted a lamp, and sat down on the bed. He remained there a long time staring into space. His mother and Alonzo Freeman had been murdered by white men for Alonzo's gold, and then Arvado had been killed for no better reason than the fact that fate had given him the same color skin as the Comanches. How could anyone be proud of belonging to the white race, and still blindly condemn all Utes because of what had happened to Nathan Meeker?

It didn't make sense, he told himself. No sense at all.

6

The news of Arvado's murder was so much of a shock to Dave that for hours he was unable to force himself to sit down with the paper and pen and write his report. Finally, close to midnight, he started, and once the words began to flow, he found that it became a release for him. When he finally finished, early morning light was tiptoeing into the room through the east window.

He capped the ink bottle and read what he had written. He had given Carl Schurz the people's reaction to the news of the fight on Milk Creek as he had seen it in Canon City, Cleora, and Gunnison, then told what Leslie had said during their talk the previous evening, ending with the major's conviction that there would be no more trouble with the Utes unless it was precipitated by the whites, and added Leslie's suggestion that the agent at Los Pinos should be replaced before Ouray died and trouble broke out there.

For a time he stared through the window at the sky above Blue Mesa that was steadily brightening with the coming day, his thoughts on Arvado and his murder, then he made a decision. He would express his real opinions to the Secretary. Perhaps he would not do any good, but at least he would give vent to his feelings.

He removed the cap from the ink bottle, dipped his pen, and wrote a violent paragraph to the effect that even Major Leslie who was as good a friend as the Utes had in Colorado realized the Indians would not be able to keep the reservation as it stood now. There was too much pressure from the press and the state's most important politicians such as Senator Henry Teller and Governor Fred-

erick Pitkin, all of them crying that "The Utes must go,"
but he said it seemed a shame that a great nation's honor
must be tarnished because white men's interest forced the
sacred word of the United States of America to be broken.
True, the Utes were only a small tribe of mountain Indians
without political power and with few friends. Still, the
only honorable course for a nation was to keep its word.
Then he capped the ink bottle a second time and went to
bed.

Dave slept until noon. When he went downstairs to
dinner, Leslie needled him about being a late sleeper, but
he apologized when Dave told him what he'd done. Leslie
said, "I'm taking a ride up the Cimarron this afternoon to
look at some cattle. I've been gone so long I don't know
what's going on. Want to ride along?"

Dave assured him he did. It was almost sundown when
they returned to find that the stage had arrived and General
Charles Adams was waiting for them in the bar. Dave and
Leslie shook hands with him, Leslie saying, "We were
expecting you. I assume you'll want to leave early in the
morning."

"By all means," Adams said. "That is, if we can't
leave tonight."

Leslie shook his head. "I think we'd be ahead to wait
until morning. We'll get our supplies together tonight and
decide what you want to do. Ouray knows you're coming
and he promised to have several of his best men go with
us. He's sent a runner after the ones who were not at the
agency, but I doubt that they'll be there until tomorrow
noon at the earliest."

"All right, we'll leave in the morning," Adams agreed.
"You've been in closer touch with the situation than I
have, but I'm sure you realize the urgency . . ."

"The urgency has to do with what Colonel Merritt
does," Leslie interrupted, a little testily, Dave thought.
"If he's moving south and chasing Indians, the women
and children will be murdered. I don't have the slightest
doubt of it."

Adams grimaced. "The Secretary is well aware of the
danger. He has already talked to President Hayes. To

General Sherman, too, I think, and an order has been sent to Merritt to hold back until we have completed the rescue of the Meeker women and Mrs. Price and her children.''

Mrs. Patrick hammered the dinner gong. Leslie rose. "We'd better go to supper. My housekeeper gets mad if we don't move when she gives the word.''

General Charles Adams was almost as interesting to Dave as Carl Schurz had been. In many ways they were alike. He thought about that as they ate supper. Adams was also a German who had fled from his homeland somewhat later than Schurz, but for the same reason. He had participated in a student revolt against the autocratic rule of the king. Like Schurz, he had fought with the Union forces against the South, then he'd come West and eventually had moved to Denver where he'd married Margaret Phelps, a sister of the wife of Colorado Territory Governor Edward McCook, and, at her insistence, had changed his name from Karl Schwanbeck to Charles Adams.

He was a big man, standing well over six feet and weighing close to two hundred and fifty pounds. He had blue eyes, a wide face, and a handsome mustache. He was, Dave thought, a striking man.

Adams had been agent at White River at one time, and later at Los Pinos, and had been able to establish a rapport with the Utes that few agents did. At the moment he was a United States Post Office Inspector of contract mail routes in both New Mexico and Colorado, a job he had been forced to leave temporarily when he received Secretary Schurz's wire to undertake the task of rescuing the Meeker women.

When they finished eating, Dave said, "I would like to go with you in the morning. I'm well enough acquainted with the Secretary to know that nothing else is going to concern him very much right now.''

"No one knows who can be useful, or even how we can," Adams said. "Rand, didn't you tell me you knew the Utes when you were growing up in the San Luis Valley?''

Dave nodded. "I didn't know any of them personally, though. Just the boy who had been raised by our neighbors.''

"You should be reminded that we may fail," Adams said. "If we do, we will very likely lose our lives. I don't doubt that many of the Indians who are holding the women and two children were my friends, but that doesn't mean they will still be my friends under these circumstances."

"I understand that," Dave said a little impatiently. "If I was overly concerned about saving my life, I wouldn't have taken this job in the first place."

"Of course not," Adams agreed. "Well then, I see no reason why you shouldn't go and I think you may be useful."

Dave went to bed a few minutes later, Leslie and Adams staying up to make plans for the trip onto the reservation. Dave was called before sunup for breakfast. Leslie gave him a bay gelding to ride, and they left with the sun not yet showing above the Blue Mesa rim to the east.

They reached Ouray's farm that afternoon, and Dave, remembering the chief as a strong and agile man in his thirties with a commanding air about him, was surprised to find him so thin that he had deep lines in his face and his buckskin suit fitted him loosely. Dave understood why Leslie had referred to him as a sick man.

Ouray was more than happy to see his old friend Adams, and for a time they talked in Spanish, then Adams introduced Dave who said, "I often saw you with your people in the San Luis Valley when I was a boy and lived with Alonzo Freeman."

Ouray nodded and smiled briefly. He spoke in Spanish. Dave did not fully understand, but it was something about Ouray remembering Alonzo Freeman and their horse trades.

Ouray took them into his adobe house. His wife, Chipeta, remained in the background, a middle-aged squaw who had lost the figure and good looks that Dave had admired when he had seen her years ago in front of a lodge on the banks of the Rio Grande.

Their home bore little resemblance to the lodge in which Ouray and Chipeta had lived years ago. It was a white man's adobe house, forty feet long and thirty feet wide. Inside was the usual white man's furniture: carpets and animal skins on the floor, brass beds, chairs, kerosene lamps, and similar trifles which didn't fit with the kind of life they had lived when Dave had been fascinated by the beehive existence that had characterized Ute villages during his boyhood years.

Dave remembered what Leslie had said that morning. "Ouray has eighty acres that's cultivated, he's got barns and a root cellar and a band of sheep and a houseful of furniture and gimcracks that would please the average Denver woman, and for what? He's not as happy as he was before he got all this stuff, but I guess he's bound to show both the Indians and the whites that a Ute can live like civilized people."

"He'll never prove it to the other Utes," Adams had said. "He's a strange and remarkable man. He's the only Indian I ever met who seems to live in two worlds, but sometimes I wonder if he feels he really belongs in either."

Dave thought about it now as he glanced around Ouray's living room. Chipeta was a good housekeeper, even judged by the average white woman's standards, but when he thought of Arvado, he wondered if Ouray and Chipeta were like him, admitting as Adams had suggested that they did not live fully in either world.

Ouray was talking to Adams in Spanish. Dave had known some of the language when he had lived on Alonzo Freeman's ranch, but he had forgotten much of it because he'd had no opportunity to use it for years. He was able to understand only part of what Ouray said, but he gathered that the Ute chief had stopped the fighting on Milk Creek by sending a white man from the Los Pinos Agency with his orders, and he had dispatched a runner to Chief Douglas's camp where the women and Mrs. Price's children were with instructions to treat the prisoners well. Now it was up to Adams and the other whites to save the three women and the two children.

Dave knew that both Adams and Leslie understood this, that Ouray was tired and sick and old in experience if not in years. He could not leave his farm. The best he could do was to offer advice, furnish guides, and keep his own Uncompahgres in line.

Late that night a runner arrived with news that Jack's

war drums were sounding on the Grand because Merritt's men were moving south from White River. There was no doubt now in Dave's mind, or in Adam's or Leslie's, that the need for haste was great. If there was another battle, the prisoners would surely be murdered. The only question now in Dave's mind was whether time had run out on them.

The rescue party, including Dave, Major Leslie, General Adams, and his personal friend Count Donhoff, a German aristocrat, and a man from the agency, left early the next morning. They were accompanied by thirteen Utes, among them Ouray's brother-in-law Sapinero and the war chief, Shavano. Dave remembered Shavano well, for he had seen him many times in the San Luis Valley. He had aged in the years since then, but not so much as Ouray.

Major Leslie drove a buckboard by which the women were to be returned to the agency. A supply wagon drawn by two mules were driven by an agency employee. The Utes were strung out on the trail, and Dave, looking at them in their black hats with the long feathers tacked to the bands, their cotton shirts and buckskin leggings, thought that time had taken away much of their individuality.

They had not been fully domesticated, but they were not the free souls they had been twelve years ago, either. It was the story of all Indians, Dave thought sadly. Their old way of life had been washed out from under them, and they had not had time to adapt themselves to the new.

The rescue party followed the Uncompahgre River and late in the afternoon reached the Gunnison. They forded it and made camp a short time later in the shadow of the great mountain known as Grand Mesa. Dave had heard it called the biggest flat-topped mountain in the world, and it could be true, he thought. They had been moving toward it all day, and Dave, intrigued by it, had given his imagination full sway.

He had amused himself with the thought that when God had created the earth, He had used His celestial tools to flatten the top of the great mountain, then had produced a

level to see that the job had been done properly. Dave had
studied the mesa all day, particularly the western edge
which dropped off precipitously. From a distance it had
reminded him of a gigantic ruler laid against the sky.

After supper Major Leslie squatted beside Dave at the
fire and lighted a cigar. He said, "Did you ever see
Sapinero before?"

"I don't think so," Dave answered. "Who is he? I
mean, is he important except for being Ouray's brother-in-
law?"

"Chances are he'll succeed Ouray as head chief," Leslie said, "but he won't be another Ouray by a damned
sight. He's important on this trip because he's Ouray's
personal representative. I wanted to tell you something that
happened quite a while ago that's hard to believe.

"Ouray was tough when he was younger, especially if
anyone questioned his authority. The story is that some of
the young bucks including Sapinero got tired of stepping to
his tune, so they decided to kill him. They had to take on
some coffin varnish before they had the guts to try it. Even
then Sapinero was the only one who didn't turn tail and
run when the time came. He tried to use an ax on Ouray
and missed, and that was almost the end of the line for
Sapinero. Ouray got him down into an irrigation ditch and
drew his knife. He'd sure as hell have cut Sapinero's heart
out if Chipeta hadn't heard her brother's howling. She ran
out and persuaded Ouray not to kill Sapinero."

Leslie laughed shortly and spread his hands. "Since
then Sapinero has been a real good Ute. I guess Ouray
trusts him as much as any of the Uncompahgres."

Dave had never heard the story, but it was reasonable
enough. Circumstances often decided human relationship.
He considered Vince Kelso, a pleasant enough man, probably honest and capable, a man he might have liked a great
deal if they had met under different circumstances.

His mind turned to Sharon Morgan. He had thought
about her many times since she had left Leslie's place on
the stage, wondering how she had made out establishing
her business and if Kelso had made any progress with her.

He wished he had written to her, but at least he would see her as soon as he returned, if he did.

He motioned toward Grand Mesa, its top lost to sight in the darkness. He asked, "Ever been up there?"

"Once," Leslie answered. "It's a beautiful country. Lots of timber and lakes. Good hunting and fishing. The Utes call it Thigunawat. The spirits of the dead Utes inhabit it. I guess we'd call it a happy hunting ground. Funny thing, though. They're not afraid to fish and hunt on it while they're alive."

"Are we going to the top from here?"

"That's not the present plan. We'll follow the rivers and take the long way around." He shrugged. "But who knows what our plans will be in another hour. If the soldiers and Jack's bunch tangle again, we might start climbing, but even if we had wings to fly up, I figure we'd be too late."

He took his cigar out of his mouth. "Funny the way things work out. Last night Ouray told us that when he first heard about the massacre and the Milk Creek fight, he considered killing himself. Everything he had tried to do for his people would be destroyed. He knows what the whites have been saying, and now they've got what they need to get the Utes moved."

He jabbed his half-smoked cigar at Dave. "Then he thought about going native and taking his Uncompahgres and joining Jack and Douglas and the rest of the White River Utes and fighting it out until they were all killed. Now that was a hell of a crazy notion, and he got over it, but it was a surprise to me that Ouray even considered it. I guess it explains why Jack and his bucks tackled Thornburgh. Jack's a smart Indian. He was raised by the Mormons, so he knows that in the long run they couldn't win, but they'd rather die here in their own country and have their spirits live up yonder on Thigunawat than be carried off in chains to Indian Territory."

"If I were a Ute," Dave said thoughtfully, "I think I would, too."

Leslie nodded. "So would I, but we're not Utes, and understanding how they feel doesn't really help solve our problem. Now, even if we get the Meeker women out alive, the question is whether they've been raped. That's what worries Adams. If they have, and if the newspapers find out, Heaven help the Utes because we sure won't be able to." He yawned and scratched the back of his neck. "I'm going to roll in. We'll be moving out early in the morning."

They were on their way before sunup, following the Gunnison River across the barren land with its occasional cedar and scattering of stunted sagebrush. Dave, staring across the country broken by innumerable arroyos to where the lower slope of Grand Mesa tipped up sharply from the valley, wondered if white men would ever make use of this land they wanted so badly.

That night they camped on the river still ten miles from its junction with the Grand. Not long after they had cooked supper, two runners rode in with word that Merritt was still moving south and Jack and his band were forted up to wait for the soldiers on Roan Plateau.

Leslie looked at Dave and nodded as if to remind him of what he had said last night. Shavano said something to Sapinero and the two Ute chiefs turned to Adams and talked for a time. Adams nodded thoughtfully, then walked slowly to where Leslie stood beside Dave on the other side of the fire.

"It's about ten miles from here to the Grand," Adams said, "and maybe thirty-five more to Plateau Creek and another fifteen to the camp where the prisoners are held. Shavano says he knows a deer trail that goes to the top of Grand Mesa from here. It might save twenty miles, but I'm not sure it's smart to take it. I mean, I don't know whether the twenty miles we'll cut off will save us any time."

Dave remembered what Adams had said about urgency the night he'd stayed at Leslie's place, and Leslie's remark about urgency depending on what Merritt did. If the soldiers were advancing, the rescuers might be too late now, and if they weren't, even a few minutes could make the difference between the life or death of the prisoners.

"Take the trail," Dave said without thinking that it was Leslie who knew the country better than the other white

men and therefore he should be the one to make the
decision. "We ought to get started tonight."

"That was my first thought," Adams agreed, "but
we'll have to leave the buckboard and supply wagon here.
From what Shavano says, the trail is a son of a bitch. It
may kill all of us and the horses."

"We'd better take the trail anyway," Leslie said thoughtfully as if only then reaching a decision. "A few hours
may be important and I believe it will save us that much."

"All right, that's what we'll do," Adams said, and
turned back to Shavano.

They started that evening. The ride to the top of Grand
Mesa was one Dave would never forget. The ascent was
sharp and they had to stop often to blow their horses; the
trail twisted around deep ravines that slashed the side of
the great mountain, following narrow shelves where a false
step or a slide would send man and horse rolling down-
ward a thousand feet.

They reached the rim before dawn and plunged into a
forest of spruce and aspen. They threaded their way through
the trees, occasionally riding across small parks that were
bright with moonlight, then finding themselves buried again
in the almost total darkness, the trees growing so close
together that riders and horses were slashed repeatedly by
branches that seemed to form a network above the trail.

Dave was reminded of what Sam Leslie had told him,
that to the Utes this flat mountain top was the home of the
spirits of their dead. They were over ten thousand feet
high, the cold breeze rattling the branches of the trees and
causing them to creak and groan, eerie sounds that made
the night more weird and threatening than it had been
during the climb.

Dave had never considered himself superstitious, yet he
could not keep the icy prickles from running up and down
his spine. Now and then the long line of riders swung
around small lakes, the moonlight touching them with
silver that seemed tremulous and unreal as the wind ruffled
the surface of the water.

They splashed across tiny streams, they heard the hooting
of owls back in the timber, the scream of some night bird

as it streaked across the sky, and later, after the moon was down and the morning light began filtering through the trees, they saw banners of mist ahead of them laying flat against the ground and giving a haunting appearance to the forest that surrounded them.

Dave wondered how many spirits of departed Ute warriors were watching them. He tried to laugh at the thought, but he could not. He was relieved when the sun finally came up and began cutting away the night chill and bringing with it a sense of normal reality to the forest.

They stopped beside a small stream and ate breakfast. Dave, squatting beside Leslie at the fire, asked, ''Did you have a feeling we were riding through a haunted country last night?''

Leslie looked startled, then grinned. ''You know, I had exactly that feeling, but I sure wasn't going to mention it to anyone. I thought I was letting my imagination get the best of me.''

''So did I,'' Dave admitted. ''Maybe I wouldn't have felt the way I did if you hadn't told me the Utes thought this was the home of the spirits of their dead.''

''I wasn't forgetting it, either,'' Leslie admitted. ''Funny thing about Indians. They see visions and hear voices, and we whites who know so damned much more than they do laugh at them and call it the superstition of savages.''

''You're saying that they know more than we do, that voices and visions are real?''

''No, you're the one who's saying it, not me.'' Leslie laughed. ''If you quoted me as saying it, folks would think I'm even crazier than I am.''

''They didn't make the ride we did,'' Dave said.

''Maybe there's something else involved that made us feel the way we did.'' Leslie paused and stroked his mustache thoughtfully, then went on, ''I couldn't keep my mind off what we might find when we get to the camp where the prisoners are. I've seen what plains Indians do to women. Rape 'em and kill 'em slow and terrible. If we find something like that, not settler women, mind you, but agency women who had an official right to be where they were, well, we'd better feel sorry for every Ute in Colorado along with the prisoners.''

''I guess we're all thinking of that,'' Dave said. ''You know, the night we stayed in Cleora, I was having a drink in the bar when I heard a freighter talking about how he'd make a good Indian out of a live one if he ever got a chance. He made me so mad I had to get out of the barroom.''

''What was his name?''

''Duke Conway.''

''Hell, I know him. He'll do it someday, too, if he gets drunk and runs into a Ute. He freights into Ouray, carrying whisky mostly, so he stays off the reservation as much as he can.''

Adams had been talking to Shavano. Now he turned to Dave and Leslie. ''Time we were moving. Shavano says we're about twelve miles from the camp.''

Dave tightened the cinch and mounted. A moment later they were under way, Shavano still leading. Dave thought about what Leslie had said. He was sure the major was right, and if the Meeker women had been abused and murdered, the innocent Utes as well as the guilty ones would pay for the crime. Ouray, Chipeta, Shavano, Sapinero, and many like them who were honestly doing all they could to keep the peace and bridge the gap between two ways of life would die or at least be banished from the ancestral homeland they loved.

The miles were gradually cut down, and Dave wondered if Shavano and Sapinero and the other Indians understood the importance of the next hour or two. About ten o'clock they rode up a ridge and reached the crest, and Adams gave the signal to stop. Directly below them in a small valley was the camp they sought.

Dave estimated there were fifteen or possibly twenty lodges in the valley. The White River Utes, less influenced by the white man's culture than the Uncompahgres, were living the same nomadic life that nearly all the Utes had followed when Dave had been a boy in the San Luis Valley.

Here was the pony herd grazing beyond the lodges just

as Dave remembered. There were a few sheep and goats, too. The boys played at being warriors, bows in their hands as they slipped through the grass in pursuit of game. On the far side of the valley a number of squaws searched for wood, and others, having found as much as they could carry, plodded back to camp.

Leslie, pulling in beside Dave, pointed to where the rim of Grand Mesa dropped away. "Yonder's Grand Valley," he said. "On the other side are the Book Cliffs. Above 'em is the Roan Plateau."

Dave nodded, remembering that was where Jack and his young men had forted up to wait for the soldiers. He wondered if they had fought another battle, and if they had, would the news have reached this camp? No men were in sight. Perhaps all of them were with Jack. Even if that were true, it did not mean necessarily that the prisoners were still alive. On occasion squaws could be as cruel and vindictive as the warriors.

Shavano had sent one of his men on down the slope to the camp. Now he loped back and said something to Shavano in Ute. The chief turned and spoke to Adams in Spanish, "Douglas and Sowerick are in a big camp on the river. They'll be back pronto."

Adams glanced at Dave and Leslie and gave a bare, half-inch nod, then he spurred his horse down the slant into the valley toward the village, Dave and Leslie following. Dave felt a great surge of excitement pound through his body. The long wait was over. Now they would know the fate of the three women and Mrs. Price's two children, and their own as well.

Adams rode past the first lodges to the last one which was a good half mile on down the valley. Dave and Leslie still followed, not knowing what to expect or what was in Adam's mind. They reined up at the last tepee and dismounted. Two squaws stood in front of the opening holding up a blanket and it occurred to Dave that at least some of the prisoners would be here.

The same thought must have been in Leslie's mind, for he said something to Adams who nodded and said, "Watch them." He turned sharply and went into the next lodge. A moment later he came out and said, "It's empty."

The three men faced the squaws, but before Adams could speak, a young white woman stepped past them. She was holding a small girl by the hand. Dave, looking at them, felt as if a great stone had just been rolled off his back, a relief so poignant that it was almost painful. If two of the prisoners were alive, the other three probably were, too.

"I'm Josephine Meeker," the young woman said. "I'm very glad to see you."

For a moment neither Adams nor the two men standing beside him could speak. Dave, his gaze on the girl, tried to swallow a lump that had appeared in his throat. He thought she looked very well to have gone through the privations that she had for the last three weeks. Her hair was cut so that it hung to her shoulders, her complexion was good, her eyes bright. She was wearing a crude coat that apparently had been cut from an annuity blanket.

Then Adams found his voice. He asked, "The other three . . . Are they all right?"

She nodded. "They're fine. I mean, they're alive and well."

Adams hesitated. Dave knew what was in his mind and that the answer was an important one. The question was hard to ask, and it took Adams a moment to think how to phrase it. He said slowly, "I know about the Utes, Miss Meeker. Did they abuse your body?"

"No," she said quickly. "They did not."

Dave saw Adams relax, as if he had some hope now for everyone who was involved in this tragedy. He said, "Thank God! We will try to get you and the rest started for home by tomorrow morning at the latest."

But it was not easy, not as easy as Adams anticipated. A short time later Douglas and Sowerick rode in from the main camp. Adams talked briefly to them, but it was plain to Dave that both chiefs were in an ugly mood.

About thirty men were gathered in Douglas's big lodge, their talk loud and threatening. Dave, following Adams, Leslie, and Sapinero into the lodge, understood enough of it to know that some of the men wanted to kill all the whites now. It would not be difficult, even if the Uncompahgres who had come with the rescue party tried to defend them. The White River Utes would not be punished any more for a dozen killings than one, so they were thinking they might just as well add the scalps of Adams and the others to the ones they already had.

The prickles began running up and down Dave's spine again as he listened to the angry talk between Douglas and Adams. The soldiers were still moving south, and in time they would reach Grand River. Douglas said the women and children would not be released until Adams stopped the soldiers. Adams said he would go north and talk to Colonel Merritt, but not until after the prisoners had been released to Major Leslie and Dave Rand and were on their way to the agency.

That was the way the talk went for five hours, back and forth, Douglas and Adams each repeating what they had said over and over, neither of them willing to give an inch. Adams had failed, Dave thought. The White River Utes didn't care what happened to the other bands. They were the ones who had stopped the soldiers and killed Major Thornburgh and a good many of his men; they had murdered Nathan Meeker and every white man at the agency. They had held three women and two small children prisoners for three weeks, and they may have raped the women.

Dave was not sure Josephine Meeker had told the truth. He had thought about what she had said and how she had said it, and he decided her answer to Adam's question had been too quick, almost as if the three women had foreseen the question and had rehearsed the answers to save their reputations.

In the end it was Sapinero who brought the talk to a head. He rose and said he'd listened long enough. He represented Chief Ouray, and Douglas and Sowerick and all of them had better know right now that if the prisoners did not arrive at Ouray's farm by the end of the week, Ouray would gather his Uncompahgres and they would release the prisoners. What was more, they'd chase the

White River Utes north into the rifles and cannons of the soldiers.

When he sat down, there was an ominous silence as Douglas and the others stared across the lodge at Sapinero and the white men. Sapinero's speech gave a new twist to the proceedings. For the first time in several hours the prickles stopped working up and down Dave's back. One thing was evident. Ouray might be a sick man, but the White River Utes were still afraid of him.

Finally Douglas broke the silence. He said to Adams, "Can you stop the soldiers?"

"I am here by the authority of President Hayes," Adams said. "As soon as the prisoners are released, I will go to see Colonel Merritt."

So a bargain was finally made. Adams would ride north to White River to see Merritt. He would take Sapinero and Sowerick and would start that night. In the morning Major Leslie and Dave and the rest of the rescue party would leave with the prisoners for the Los Pinos Agency.

When the white men left Douglas's lodge, they met Mrs. Meeker and Mrs. Price who were coming from the willows along the creek where they had been hidden. Josephine Meeker was with them. Behind them was a pleasant-faced squaw carrying Mrs. Price's small son on her back. The little girl ran beside them in the grass. The children at least had been treated well, Dave thought, but that was not surprising. That was the way the Utes were.

Mrs. Meeker was very thin, the color gone from her face, and she limped as she walked. Dave learned later that she had received a shallow bullet wound in the thigh at the time of the massacre. Mrs. Price, wearing a garment similar to Josephine Meeker's, looked placid and well fed. Once more Dave gave a great sigh of relief. They weren't out of the woods yet, but this could have been, he thought, so very much worse.

Adams shook hands with Mrs. Meeker and told her about the agreement which had been made. She tried to smile, tried to thank him, but it was hard for her to talk. Dave, thinking of the horror of the massacre at the White River Agency, and the constant danger that had been their daily companion, wondered how the three women had retained their sanity.

The white men had little chance to talk to the women that night because some of the Utes were always around. Many of them knew a good deal of English, and Adams told Dave and Leslie that if the Indians got the notion he was investigating the murder at the agency, they might still all be killed. But they did learn that the women had been treated reasonably well, the weather had been good except for a hailstorm and a windy night that had made them uncomfortable.

The Indians had shifted camps seven times as Merritt had pushed south, and it was in Dave's mind that they had reached this camp barely in time. If the soldiers had kept coming, there was not much more room left in which the Utes could retreat. He still thought that if the showdown had been forced before the rescue party arrived, the prisoners would have been killed.

Before Adams left that night, he had a moment alone with Mrs. Price. He started to ask her the same question he had asked Josephine, and she said quickly, too quickly he told Dave and Leslie, that nothing of the sort had happened.

"I don't know," he said. "I just don't know, but I hope the damned newspapers don't get hold of any rumors about what was done to the women."

After supper Adams rode north toward Colonel Merritt's camp. He was accompanied by Sapinero and Count Donhoff. In the morning Dave and Leslie left the camp with the prisoners and the Uncompahgres. There was a good chance, Dave thought, that the White River Utes would change their minds about letting the prisoners go, or that the party might be attacked on their way across Grand Mesa, but the trip back to Ouray's farm was uneventful.

The prisoners were welcomed by Ouray, who was plainly relieved to see them alive and in good health. Chipeta turned her house over to them, and cried a little, perhaps in relief, too. It seemed to Dave that Mrs. Meeker was as astonished to find Ouray and Chipeta living like white people as by anything that had happened.

Mrs. Meeker was also surprised to be met at Ouray's

farm by her son, Ralph Meeker, who was in New York when he heard about the massacre. A short time later Secretary Schurz appointed him a special agent of the Interior Department and he had come West at once.

Dave and Major Leslie shook hands with Ralph Meeker and rode upriver to the Los Pinos Agency where Dave met the agent, Wilson M. Stanley. The smell of whisky was strong about him, and Dave's first thought was that he should be removed before trouble broke out here. That, Dave remembered, had been Leslie's suggestion.

Dave remained at the agency for a time while Leslie went on with Ralph Meeker and the women and two children to Lake City. He turned back at that point, the others going to Alamosa where they boarded the narrow gauge for Denver and from there continued north to their home in Greeley.

When he was at Ouray's farm Dave had written a telegram informing Secretary Schurz that the Meeker women had been rescued and were safe, that they were under Ouray's protection, and asked for instructions. He added that a detailed report would follow by mail, and signed the telegram, Dave Rand, Special Agent. He asked Ouray for a runner who took it to Lake City. From there it was wired to Washington.

After he reached the agency he spent hours on the report, giving Schurz as complete an account as he could of what had happened from the time General Adams had arrived at Leslie's place on the Cimarron to the present. This went out by mail. Dave was still at the agency when Adams returned with Donhoff and Sapinero, and Leslie got back from Lake City.

Adams told Dave and Leslie about talking to Merritt, and not being trusted by either the Indians or the soldiers, and Merritt's resentment at being held back from going after the murderers by that "Damned Dutch Secretary." At least the fighting had not started again and the prisoners had been rescued, so Adams's mission had been successful.

At the agency Adams found a telegram from Schurz saying that the White River Utes were to move their camp to somewhere near the Los Pinos Agency, that a commission consisting of Adams, General Hatch, and Ouray was to try to determine who was the guilty of the murders at White River and the guilty parties were to be dealt with as white men would have been.

This gratified Dave and Leslie as well as Adams because it was a definite step forward for Indians to be dealt with as white men. But Leslie shook his head. He said, "You're going to have a hell of a hard time finding out who's guilty. They won't tattle on each other, and the Meeker women weren't really sure who done the killing. Besides, the Utes won't accept any testimony given by women."

"I know," Adams said glumly. "But we've got Ouray on the commission. He'll get it out of them if anybody can."

"And if he doesn't?" Dave asked.

"I don't know." Adams rubbed his face with his big hands. "The hounds are in full cry now. Governor Pitkin. Senator Teller. William Byers through the columns of the *News*. All the small-time politicians and editors to boot. You'd think the only words they know are 'The Utes must go.' Right now I doubt that Ouray can save anything."

"I think he knows it," Leslie said.

"The innocent Utes will be pushed out of the state along with the guilty," Dave said bitterly. "I don't think the danger is over. If Ouray thought about going native and fighting till he died, he'll think about it again, and the fact that the White River Utes whipped the soldiers at Milk Creek will encourage them to try."

"Well, we'll see," Adams said gloomily.

The next day Adams left to catch the train at Alamosa and Leslie returned to his ranch on the Cimarron. Dave stayed at the agency for a time, but he was at Ouray's farm when a wire came from Schurz directing him to remain at Los Pinos for the hearings. This gave him a few days, perhaps a week, that were free. Early the next morning he left for the mining camp of Ouray.

7

Dave rode the thirty-odd miles upstream to Ouray, arriving late in the afternoon. The valley had narrowed, then widened, and narrowed again, and then he found that he was in town, the mountains all around. The mining camp was located in a small park, the most beautiful site for a town he had ever seen. As he rode up the sloping Main Street, he looked at the mountain wall in front of him and wondered how even a man on foot could get through it.

The day was a bitterly cold one, with about six inches of snow on the ground. There had been no snow at Ouray's farm, but that was nearly two thousand feet lower than here. He left his horse in a livery stable and, stepping into a store, bought a heavy coat. He was chilled to the bone, the mackinaw that had been adequate at the agency and Ouray's farm had felt paper thin for the last five miles of his ride.

His next stop was the hotel where he was lucky enough to find a room, then he asked about Sharon's shop. The clerk hesitated as if it wasn't a decent subject to talk about, and Dave wondered if she had done something in the short time she had been here to tarnish her reputation.

Or maybe Vince Kelso had done something. As he stood waiting for the clerk to answer him, the thought about Kelso raised such a heat of fury in him that he clenched his fists until the knuckles were white. If it were true, he would settle with Kelso the next time he saw him.

The clerk finally decided to tell him, even stepping to the door and pointing out the direction. She worked in her house, he said, just two blocks off Main Street. Darkness was almost complete by the time he left the hotel, lamplight falling through cabin windows onto the snow so that the little town, shadowed by the towering peaks around it, had a haunting, storybook appearance.

He walked the two blocks rapidly and made the turn at the corner as the clerk had directed, the snow crunching noisily under his boots. Then he was standing in front of her house, a log cabin set close to the street.

He saw her sitting in the front room, doing some kind of sewing, the lamplight falling on her face. He had carried a mental image of her from the last moment he had seen her in the stage at Sam Leslie's place, and now he thought she was even more striking than he remembered. She was wearing a blue dress that went well with her coloring. Her blond hair hung in two long curls down her back and made her look younger than he remembered her.

He knocked. When she opened the door, the warm air rushed at him and he knew she must feel the cold air, but he didn't want to step inside until she asked him. He said, "Hello, Sharon," and waited.

The light was so thin that she did not recognize him for a moment. She stood staring at him, bundled up in his heavy coat, his broad-brimmed hat pulled low over his forehead. Apparently she identified his voice, for suddenly she squealed, "Dave," and caught him by both arms and pulled him into the room. "Why didn't you tell me who you were?" She shut the door, then threw her arms around him and hugged him. "Oh Dave, you're like a warm ray of summer sunshine and just as welcome."

He hugged her and wanted to kiss her, but it was not the right time, he thought. He did not know how she felt about him, or about Vince Kelso, for that matter, and he guessed he didn't really know how he felt about her. He must not forget, he warned himself, that they were both strangers in a strange land and they were lonely, so their feelings at this particular moment were not to be trusted.

"Take off your hat and coat," she said. "This is the nicest thing that's happened to me since I've come to Ouray. I've wondered so often what you were doing and what happened to you, and why I haven't heard from you."

"I'll have to admit I've thought of you a time or two," he said, smiling.

She laid his coat across a cutting table and placed his hat upon it. She said, "This is the woman part of the house. Or should I say the business part? Anyhow, we're not going to stay here."

Sharon picked up the lamp and started toward the kitchen. Dave hesitated, glancing around the room. It was the first time for weeks he had been in a white woman's house, and it struck him that even the smell here was different than he had been used to. Perhaps the odor came from the dress goods piled on one end of the cutting table. Somewhere she had secured a sewing machine which must have been very expensive. She also has a dressmaker's dummy, and on the other side of the room there was a pile of hatboxes, the top one covered by two long purple plumes.

"Come on," she said impatiently. "I've been working on a shirtwaist all afternoon until my eyes are about to pop out of my head. I'm glad to get out of this room."

When he followed her into the kitchen, he saw that the room was more than a kitchen. A stove, table, chairs, and shelves filled with groceries were on one side of the room, and on the other was a divan, a marble-topped stand, and a rocker with a pink cushion on the seat and an antimacassar pinned to the back.

She motioned to the divan. "Sit down, Dave. Or take the rocker if you think it would be more comfortable. And don't tell me you've had supper because I'm going to cook for both of us. If you have eaten, you'll just have to eat again."

"I haven't, but I didn't intend to mooch a meal . . ."

"You hush that up," she said. "I'll cook a better supper for you than you can find anywhere else in town. Besides, I haven't cooked for a man in a long time." She laughed. "Not for a week since Vince left with a load of freight for some mine."

Dave's heart jumped. He said more sharply than he intended, "Is he hanging around here? I mean, is he bothering you?"

"No, he hasn't been bothering me." She laughed again as if enjoying the disturbance she had created in Dave. "Except to ask me to marry him, but I haven't accepted. I'm waiting for you to ask me, then I'll have a choice."

He sat down on the divan, wondering if she was serious. She built up her fire, set the coffeepot on the stove, and began stirring up a batch of biscuits. He said, "I don't know about you, Sharon. You never struck me as being a frivolous woman. Or a forward one, either."

"But I sound like a forward one, don't I?" She laughed, a spontaneous sound that he liked to hear. "Why, I guess I am forward, all right, but never frivolous. You'll just have to get used to me because I can't change." She glanced over her shoulder at him, still laughing. "But you can change, can't you, Dave? Maybe I'll marry you. Who knows? I'll have to see how much you need changing. You see, that's why a woman marries a man. If she can't improve him, there's no need to marry him."

"All right," he said testily, irritated with himself for thinking she was serious. "Now that you've had your fun, tell me the truth. Has Vince asked you to marry him?"

She turned, holding her dough-smeared hands up in front of her. For a moment she looked directly at him, then went back to the biscuits. "Yes, he has asked me to marry him, but I haven't given him an answer. I just don't feel that I know him well enough."

"You don't," Dave said, "although when you think about our stage ride, it seems that we got to know each other pretty well for the few days we were together."

"Yes, we did," she agreed, "but for me marriage is forever. Vince gets impatient with me when I say that, but I tell him I've got to be sure." She rolled out her biscuits with quick, expert movements, jabbed her cutter into the dough and laid the round pieces into the pan until she covered the bottom. "How did you find out where I was?"

"I asked at the hotel."

She washed her hands in a basin on the back of the stove, dried them, and slid the pan into the oven. She said with a trace of bitterness, "I suppose the clerk told you I was a bad woman who lost her reputation the first week she was here."

"No, he didn't say that. Why should he?"

"It's like Vince said on the stage. There aren't enough good women in Ouray who want hats and dresses made to keep me working. I found that out the first few days I was here, so I moved next to the red-light district. That convinced some of the respectable people that I belong in this part of town. The truth is I'm just working for the bad women, and the surprising thing is that as far as my relations with them are concerned, they are not as bad as most people think. Some of them are unhappy girls who don't know what else to do. I feel sorry for them."

He nodded, thinking that was understandable. He said, "I suppose they give you lots of business."

"All I can do," she said. "Fine dresses are a business investment with them. They're good pay, too. Now let's talk about you. What have you been doing since I saw you? It's been a month, hasn't it?"

"Close to it," he agreed, and told her about the rescue of the Meeker women as she finished supper.

She called him to the table then and they began to eat, Sharon remaining silent as if preoccupied about something. Glancing at her, he sensed a girlish immaturity about her that he had not felt on the stage and it disturbed him. For some reason she was determined to make her own living here in Ouray, and he wondered why.

Presently she said, "I read about the rescue in the Ouray *Times,* but it didn't tell everything. It must have been exciting."

"There were a few times when I was a little scared," he admitted.

"But you defend them," she burst out. "Dave, how can you?"

He was angry then. This was a subject he had intended to avoid, but she seemed determined to force an argument. He held his answer for a time until he was certain he could control his feelings, then he asked mildly, "Why do you want to argue about it?"

The question confused her. She rose and, bringing the coffeepot from the stove, filled his cup. When she returned to her chair, she said, "I'm sorry, Dave. I didn't intend to start another argument like we had on the stage. I've always been ashamed of that, and I wouldn't have blamed you if you never came to see me." She hesitated, then asked, "But I still want to know why you defend them."

"I don't defend the White River Utes who murdered Nathan Meeker and his men. They should be punished and I think they will be. A commission has been appointed to hold hearings at the agency and try to find out who is guilty."

"I see," she said carefully.

"The only thing that makes me mad is the idea that *all* the Utes who live in Colorado should be punished for what a handful of them did at White River. Ouray and Chipeta live like white people. You could never find a nicer couple than they are. A lot of the others are decent and law-abiding, too. Take Ouray's brother-in-law, Sapinero. He stood up in Douglas's lodge and looked him in the eyes and made him back down. We weren't armed, and we were outnumbered about seven or eight to one. They could have wiped us out in a matter of seconds. If Sapinero hadn't said what he did, I don't think we would have rescued the prisoners."

"I see," she said again. "Were the women"—she hesitated, then forced herself to say the word—"outraged?"

"They said not. General Adams asked Josephine Meeker and Mrs. Price."

He looked across the table at Sharon, a little sick with the knowledge that suddenly the good warm feeling had deserted them. Here was a subject upon which they would never agree, a subject that must be skirted if they were to get along with each other.

He rose. "I'd better get back to the hotel. You're tired, and I got up early this morning. Thanks for the supper. You don't know how good it is to taste fine cooking after eating camp fare and the slop I've been having at the agency."

She rose and came around the table. "I'm going to be

forward again," she said, and put her arms around him.
She tipped her head back to look up at him, and went on,
"I knew this was something we shouldn't mention and I
didn't intend to bring it up, but it was just popped out. I've
been so sorry for the Meeker women and Mrs. Price. I
didn't think you'd find them alive. Or if you did, I was
sure they would have been abused." She swallowed, then
added, "I think you and Major Leslie and General Adams
and the rest were very brave to go after them."

"I didn't feel very brave," he said.

"Let's try again tomorrow night," she said. "Come for
supper. I hate to eat by myself."

"All right," he said. "I'll bring the groceries."

She nodded, smiling brightly, the tears very close. "That
would be fine if you want to. Please come earlier. I don't
have any work that's pushing me."

She still had her arms around him, her head was still
tipped back. Suddenly his intentions were forgotten and he
kissed her. It was not the perfunctory good-bye kiss she
had given him when she'd left the Leslie place; it shocked
him and roused him when he found her lips answering his.
He shoved her away from him because he knew he had to.

"I'm sorry," he said. "I didn't intend to do that."

He walked into the front room and put on his coat. He
picked up his hat and moved to the door. She had followed
him and had set the lamp on the cutting table. Now she
asked in a low tone, "Why, Dave?"

He stopped, right hand on the doorknob. "Why what?"
he asked.

"Why are you sorry you kissed me?"

His hand dropped to his side, a wry smile on his lips. "I
think I'm in love with you, Sharon, but I don't want to
hurry it. I hope you will wait a little while with Vince,
too. I feel like you do, that marriage is forever."

"I'll wait," she said. "Good night, Dave."

"Good night, Sharon," he said, and left the house.

He walked to the hotel through the sharp, bracing air.
The glittering stars in the patch of sky framed by the peaks
seemed to be closer than he had ever seen them before. As

he walked, the snow crunched underfoot, reminding him of the winters he had lived with Alonzo Freeman, the good boyhood years that had fled into the past. He could never return to them again, and then the thought came to him that perhaps he had never really let go of them or he would not be so cautious with Sharon, that maybe he shrank from the responsibility of having a wife and children.

No, that wasn't true, he told himself. He had been exposed to a number of women who would have married him if he'd asked them. Some had been cheap. Others had been hypocrites, pretending to be one thing when they were quite another. And there had been a few in Washington who had encouraged him with every sly feminine trick known to women since the day when wisdom had come to Eve. He had eluded them largely because he felt they had a wrong set of standards. To him Washington society was frivolous and false, and he wanted no part of it.

He stopped a block from the hotel and stared at the stars that were so bright and shimmering in this thin, frosty air. His hands, jammed into his pockets, were fisted so tightly that his nails dug into his palms. Why, he was a fool. Of course he loved Sharon. Compared to the other women he had known, she stood out like one of the great peaks that imprisoned Ouray in its little park.

If he had any sense he would go back and tell her and ask her to marry him. But he didn't. Only one thing stopped him, her harsh and condemning attitude toward the Utes. As he resumed his walk to the hotel, he wasn't sure it was important, but he thought it was. Such blindness would come only from hate, and yet hate didn't fit with the other qualities he had found in her and which he admired.

He stepped into the hotel bar and bought a handful of cigars, then had a drink, hoping that whisky would settle the uneasiness in him, but it did not. He climbed the stairs to his room and smoked a cigar, then went to bed, but he did not sleep for a long time. Suddenly he remembered that he had not asked where Vince Kelso was or what he was doing.

He realized then he was jealous of the man. That was a
hell of a note, he told himself gloomily. He wasn't sure he
wanted Sharon, but he couldn't stand the thought that she
might be in love with Vince Kelso and in the end would
marry him.

Dave came to Sharon's front door in the tag end of the
afternoon, the light still strong enough for him to read the
sign beside her front door: MILLINERY AND DRESSMAKING,
ORDERS FILLED PROMPTLY.

She had courage, he thought, and a great sense of inde-
pendence to live this way and in this part of town. She
must also have a fine disregard for public opinion, a trait
which he admired and had seldom found in women.

When she opened the door, he handed the sack of
groceries to her, saying, "Let me knock some of the snow
off my boots. I think I packed some in last night."

"It won't hurt anything," she said.

He pulled the door shut and kicked against the casing
with one boot and then the other. When he stepped inside,
he saw that she had gone on into the kitchen with the
groceries. He draped his coat across the cutting table, laid
his hat on the coat, and followed her.

She seemed subdued, he thought, as she glanced at him,
her eyes searching his face as if trying to discover his
feelings. He said, "It's been a pleasure looking forward to
eating another one of your good meals."

"Don't you think of anything except your stomach?"
she asked tartly.

"Are there other things to think about?" he asked.

She laughed in spite of herself. "Why, yes there are,"
she said.

"Where is Vince and what's he doing?" Dave asked.
"I aimed to find out last night and I guess I forgot it. All I
remember you saying is that he was freighting to some
mine."

"That's about all I know," she said. "I've forgotten
which one, but I do remember that it's high and quite a
ways from here. I thought he would be back before now,
but this snow may have stopped them."

"Them?"

She hesitated, then said, "He's working for Duke Conway."

"Duke Conway." He shouted the words at her, unable to believe he'd heard right. "Are you sure?"

"I'm sure," she said, smiling slightly. "He said you'd take it that way."

"What's the matter with him?" Dave demanded. "He saw Conway at Cleora. He knows what kind of man he is. Major Leslie knows him and says he's . . ."

He stopped, realizing that a tirade directed at Sharon would not do any good. She said, "I don't want you to think I'm trying to defend him. He's big enough to defend himself and it's his business who he works for, but there are two things you should know. One is that the job he expected to get was taken before he got here. The second is that during the winter it's hard to find work. From what he said, I judge this freighting job is a dangerous one and nobody but a crazy man like Conway would even take it."

"Well, it's like you say. It's his business who he works for."

"Yes, I think it is. Dave, go ahead and smoke. I don't mind. My father smoked all the time."

"Thank you," he said. "I will if it won't bother you."

He took a cigar from his coat pocket, bit off the end, and lighted it. He was silent as she cooked supper, thinking about Vince Kelso. Dave remembered that the man had said he was nearly broke, so when he arrived and found the job gone that he had expected to have, it was only natural that he would take anything that came came along. Still, working for Duke Conway . . .

Dave shrugged and put Kelso out of his mind. He had pleasanter things to think about while he was with Sharon. He watched her move around the stove to the table. She was quick and graceful and feminine, her body round and soft even though she was an unusually long-legged girl who was taller than average.

Sharon needed a tall husband, he told himself. Well, both Kelso and he were tall enough to qualify. Even in her kitchen she retained what he called the regal bearing he had noticed when they were traveling together. She was a strong girl, he thought, both in spirit and in body. Even here in a rough mining camp life would not conquer her.

There was another quality about her that he liked. He could relax with her as long as they stayed away from the Indian problem. Usually he was ill at ease with a woman. He felt different with Sharon. She was open and honest, and he did not have to be careful of every word that he said. It was fun simply to be with her.

"Is there something wrong with me tonight?" she asked. "You sit there looking at me as if I had three ears."

"No," he said, smiling slightly. "It's just that I enjoy watching you."

She turned to see if he were being facetious. Deciding that he wasn't, she said, "I suppose I should be complimented."

"You should indeed," he said.

She gave him a curtsy. "Thank you, kind sir. I do not find that multitudes of men stand around admiring me."

"I am thankful for small favors such as little competition," he said, thinking that she was paying a greater price for locating here than she had expected.

A short time later she announced that supper was ready. After they ate and had washed and dried the dishes, they sat on the divan, Dave smoking and Sharon holding some fancy work on her lap. She stared at it, leaving the needle stuck through the cloth where it was tightened by the hoop.

"Dave," she said, "I want to tell you about myself. It won't be easy, but I've got to do so you'll understand why I'm not exactly rational on the subject of Ute Indians. I didn't intend to quarrel that time on the stage and I had promised myself I wouldn't let it come up last night, but it did. I've thought about it ever since and I've decided I want to tell you why I am that way. I don't suppose it will make any real difference except that you'll know it isn't just prejudice or a feminine whim."

He took her hand that was next to him. She did not

draw it away, but sat with her gaze on her fancy work. He said, "All right, let's have your autobiography."

She gave him a quick smile that faded immediately. She said, "I don't like to talk about myself and I don't do it very often, so it won't be easy. My parents were fifty-niners. I was three years old when they came to Denver, so I don't remember much about it. Not the first year, anyway, but from what Dad used to tell me times were pretty hard and they almost starved to death that winter, with prices so high and work hard to find. My father's brother Ben was with them. He was much younger than my father, just a boy when they came, so my folks actually raised him and he was like a brother to me.

"I have one sister named Meg. She's Ben's age and because she's older than I am, she bossed me around. We quarreled all the time and Ma took her part. I hated her. Sometimes I'm ashamed of myself when I stop and think how much I hated her while we were growing up.

"We lived on a farm on the South Platte just below Denver. Dad raised potatoes and he made a small fortune. He said he'd dig his gold out of the ground, all right, but he wouldn't go up into the mountains to do it.

"My mother died when I was sixteen. I'm ashamed to admit it, but I wasn't sorry. Maybe I was really glad she was gone. When she was alive I was a sort of glorified servant. Meg got the nice clothes and the holidays and the best bedroom in the house. She had three or four men who wanted to marry her. After Ma died, she did marry one of them and went East with him. I don't hear from her very often. The last time was Christmas.

"Dad sold his farm and bought a cattle ranch on the plains east of Denver. Uncle Ben stayed with us and I kept house. I didn't realize it then, but those were the happiest years of my life. I think they were for Dad, too. He seemed in better health and he loved working with cattle. He would have sold the farm sooner than he did, but Ma wouldn't let him. She always said she wasn't a gambler and the farm was a sure thing. She bossed all of us except Meg, even Uncle Ben.

"I had my own horse, a pinto named Sparks. I rode a lot, and sometimes I helped work the cattle with Dad and Uncle Ben. If I'd had my druthers, we'd have gone on forever that way, but it was too good to last. Dad was thrown from his horse and killed. After that neither Ben nor I wanted to live there, so we sold the ranch and moved to Denver.

"Ben couldn't live in town. He told me he'd find a place and send for me. He was gone about a month when he wrote that he'd found it in Middle Park on the Grand River. Good hunting and fishing and a wonderful cattle range. He said he'd build a log house with a room for me, and I was to take all of our money out of the bank and bring it with me when I came. We'd stock the range and we'd buy some good saddle horses, and we'd have everything just the way we wanted."

For the first time she looked at him and he saw that the tears were very close. She turned her head to stare at the fancy work on her lap again and went on, "I had one more letter from him saying I'd have to wait for a while, that the Indians were getting pretty mean. They'd been setting fires in the timber and the forest fires were awfully bad. Sometimes the Indians burned a settler out or stole his horses, and although he didn't expect any serious trouble, he thought I'd better not come till they settled down.

"I had been working in a millinery shop and I just couldn't stand being cooped up in a city any longer. I wrote to him that I'd take my chances with the Indians and for him to let me know as soon as he had a house for me to live in. I never heard from him again, but a neighbor wrote that a band of Utes who rode past his place were mad about something. They saw him working on the house, so they shot him."

She couldn't go on. He put an arm around her and brought her to him, and for a long time she sat motionless, her head on his shoulder. He said finally, "I understand how you feel. I don't suppose that the guilty Indians were punished."

"Of course not," she said. "They never are. The ones

who murdered Nathan Meeker won't be, either. You'll see.''

"I still don't understand why you blame the Uncompahgre Utes," he said. "They have a right to their land regardless of what the others have done.''

He knew at once he shouldn't have said it. She drew away from him and sat straight-backed and stiff. The murder of her uncle must have been such a shock to her that she could not even talk about the Indian question coherently, he thought.

"You don't have to talk about it any more," he said. "I shouldn't have brought it up.''

"No, it's all right," she said. "I've got to get over the way I feel. You see, I might as well not have a sister as far as any family goes. Uncle Ben was something special because he was all I had. He had been like a brother to me as long as I could remember. It wasn't as if he had died the way Dad did, or if he'd got smallpox or mountain fever or something. He never hurt the Utes. He was just murdered, Dave. Don't you see? If Ouray is such a great chief and a friend of the white men, why did he let it happen?''

There was no use to explain to her that Ouray living here on the Uncompahgre could not possibly control the young men of Douglas's or Jack's band, and it would only have made her furious to say that if Nathan Meeker and the rest of the whites, who had not dealt honestly or fairly with the White River bands, had been fair and reasonable, all this trouble would never have happened.

"Ouray wasn't there, Sharon," he said. "I'm sorry about your uncle.''

She rose, too restless to sit still. She said, "Let me warm the coffee up.''

"No, it's time I was getting back to the hotel." He rose and faced her, and then impulsively he took her into his arms and kissed her. This time he did not tell her he was sorry, but when he let her go, he said, "I do understand the way you feel, Sharon.''

"I won't ever talk to you about it again," she said. "I had to tell you so you would know. Now you do.''

"May I come to see you again tomorrow night?"

"Please do," she said. "I'll try to be better company. And Dave, when you write those articles for your newspaper, tell the people back East that no one has any right to criticize us in Colorado until they have lived out here and know from their own experience what it's like."

"I'll try to get it said," he promised.

As he walked back to the hotel through the chill night air, he wondered if he should have told her why he was out here. No, this was not the night, he decided, but he would have to tell her sometime and it would not be easy.

8

Dave was playing poker in the hotel bar the following afternoon when he felt a hard slap on his shoulder, and heard a man say, "Damned if it ain't the philosopher. You never know what you're going to run into in a mining camp."

Dave turned to see Vince Kelso grinning at him. He was dressed in an immaculate blue serge suit, his black mustache was neatly clipped as usual, and although he smelled of bay rum and obviously had shaved recently, his face was still dark with stubble.

"Vince!" Dave slapped Kelso on the back and shook hands. "It's only fair to tell you I hate you, but it's good to see a familiar mug like yours."

"I hate you, too," Kelso said amiably, "and it's good to see your mug, even if it is ugly."

"Wait'll I cash in," Dave said, "and I'll buy you a drink."

"You bet I'll wait for that," Kelso said, still grinning. "I'll mooch a drink off a rich newspaperman every chance I get."

A moment later Dave led the way to the bar and ordered whisky and offered Kelso a cigar. He said, "Sharon tells me you're working for Duke Conway."

"I was down to see Sharon a little while ago and she told me you raised hell when you heard it," Kelso said. "Then she says you two finally agreed it wasn't none of your business, which it ain't, but I'll tell you how it was. With the Injun scare and all, the feller who promised me a job figured I wasn't coming, so he hired another man. What with the bad weather coming on, a lot of mines had closed down and here I was, broke with no prospects. Along comes Conway needing a man to help him get a load of freight up to the Fairy Queen and offered me the job. I'd rather work for a son of a bitch than starve, so I took the job.''

"I suppose he still wants to kill Indians.''

Kelso's face turned grave. "He does for a fact, Dave. You'n me don't see eye to eye on the Indian proposition, but I don't see it the way Conway does, either. There ain't no sense in kicking a dog if he's asleep. When we were in Cleora, I thought Conway's big gab was mostly whisky talk, but you know, I think he really would shoot an Indian if he had a chance.''

"He's crazy,'' Dave said sourly.

"Crazy as a loon and strong as a bull,'' Kelso said. "He'll take chances no sane man would think about and he gets the job done. I'm going out to Canon City with him in a day or two, and if we don't get snowed in, we'll have another load of freight in here before Christmas.''

"You'll never make it,'' Dave said.

Kelso shrugged. "Maybe not, but he pays good, so I'll go along.'' He picked up his glass and drank and shook his head when Dave offered another. "I'm having supper with you'n Sharon. I figure one drink's enough. You'll probably make a fool out of me in front of Sharon again, and an extra drink won't help.''

"You never forgot that, did you?'' Dave asked irritably.

"You bet I didn't,'' Kelso answered. "She's my kind of woman and I want her. I don't think you're the right man for her.''

"Why?''

"You're a newspaperman, ain't you? You'll be traveling from hell to breakfast, leaving her and your kids at home.'' He shook his head. "She deserves a home with a man in it.''

"I suppose your freighting will keep you at home.''

Kelso shook his head. "No, but it's just a job. I'm figuring to save a little. Come spring, I'll find some other kind of work.''

Dave took his cigar out of his mouth and turned it in his

fingers. He said thoughtfully, "Vince, it's a real strange deal. Sharon didn't say so, but I get the feeling that if it wasn't for you, I'd have clear sailing."

"The same goes for me," Kelso said. "I've asked her to marry me till I'm tired of saying the words, and all I get is some crazy answer about waiting until she's sure and marriage being forever. Well, I can wait for a while, but I never won no medals for patience. The way I feel about her, I've got to know pretty soon."

Dave nodded. "I know how you feel. If you hadn't got on the stage that time in Canon City . . ."

"I've thought the same thing about you," Kelso interrupted. "Yes, sir, if I had her to myself, I think we'd be married by now." He waggled a finger at Dave. "And another thing. You don't know how close I came to not taking that stage. I was as scared as anybody in Canon City, but I said to myself that I wasn't gonna let no Eastern dude bluff me. I didn't know I was gonna want to marry the girl, but I figured I wasn't gonna be pushed out by you on general principles, so I climbed in and prayed my hair would stay on my head."

"Well, you didn't lose it." Dave put his cigar back into his mouth and pulled on it, then he said thoughtfully, "I've often wondered why Sharon came. She was scared, too. I think she'd be the first to admit it."

"I don't know," Kelso said. "I've thought about it, but I don't think it was just because she was in a hurry about getting her shop started and didn't want to spend her money sitting in a Canon City hotel like she said. She never told me how much money she's got, but I think it's plenty."

"I have the same idea," Dave agreed.

"Have you asked her to marry you?"

"No."

Kelso sighed. "Sometimes I think she likes you better'n me. Why don't you go ahead and ask her? If she says yes, I'll step out and not bother her no more."

"I'm not quite ready," Dave said, "but I will when I think the time's right. I've got a hunch she's having fun with both of us."

"Yeah, I think you're right," Kelso said moodily, "but it don't make me no never mind. I still love her. I've watched her since she got here, getting the cold shoulder from the 'respectable women,' but she went right ahead and got her business started." He slapped his palm against the cherrywood bar. "But it's like I told you once. I know how these mining camps are. It's hell on a single woman like Sharon. She's just plain lonesome. I'd like to get her out of here."

"If she was married," Dave said, "I suppose the good women would accept her."

Kelso nodded. "I think they would. The way it is now they think the worst of her."

"I'm going upstairs and shave," Dave said. "Want to wait for me?"

"I'll be here," Kelso said.

When Dave joined him half an hour later, Kelso had a bottle of champagne in his hand. "I thought we'd celebrate," he said. "Three lonely stage passengers getting together again in a valley of strangers."

"Good idea," Dave said. "I wish I'd thought of it."

That night Sharon's supper was up to her usual high standard. After the meal was eaten, she drank champagne with the two men, but somehow Dave sensed a restraint that was unusual with her. He wondered if she was measuring one against the other, perhaps calculating which would make the better husband. He was ashamed of the thought immediately and knew he was doing her an injustice.

After the dishes had been washed and dried and put away, and most of the champagne drunk, Kelso said suddenly as if he had only then thought of it, "Sharon, it ain't no secret that both of us are in love with you and want to marry you. You've put me off and Dave says he ain't asked you, but he's going to."

He was stupid, Dave thought angrily, or he'd had too much champagne. Dave said, "We'd better thank the lady and leave, Vince. It's been a good evening. Let's not spoil it."

"I ain't spoiling nothing," Kelso said. "I just want to know how I stand."

Sharon was pressing hard against the back of her rocking chair, startled and embarrassed. She said, "Dave's right, Vince, I'm pretty tired."

He ignored her. He rattled on, "I tell you what, Sharon. Dave'n me had a talk before we came down this evening, and we agreed that if the other fellow hadn't got into the stage in Canon City that morning, the one who did would have married you by now. Why don't we just cut cards to see who gets you? The other one'll drop out and give the winner a clear field."

For a moment she stared at him as if she could not believe he actually had said it, then she was furious. She stood up, her lips quivering, her angry gaze moving from one to the other. She burst out, "So you talk about me and decide you're going to gamble for me as if I were one of the common women in the next block. Well, I'm not. I won't be gambled for, and the way I feel right now I wouldn't marry either one of you if you got down on your knees and crawled from here to Denver. Now get out of here, both of you."

"Wait a minute," Kelso said. "You can't . . ."

"Get out," she screamed.

Dave was angry then. Suddenly she had become a hoyden, a side of her he had not seen before. He said, "I don't know why you're running me out. It wasn't my idea to cut the cards to see . . ."

"It doesn't make any difference," she cried. "You two get together and talked about me, didn't you? You decided that all you had to do was to figure out which one would have me. Well, I'll tell you something about a woman. About this woman, anyway. She makes up her own mind who she is going to marry and no man is going to make it up for her."

Dave rose from the divan and walked to the door into her work room, then he turned. She was looking at him, not Kelso who was still seated on the divan. He thought he had never seen her more beautiful than she was at that moment, her cheeks flaming with color, her eyes sparkling with the fury that possessed her.

"Thanks for supper, Sharon," he said. "You know you're very pretty when you're mad."

"Get out," she cried. "Damn you, just get out. I never want to see either one of you again."

Dave went on into the work room and put on his coat. He heard her yell something at Kelso, then a pan banged against the wall and Kelso came through the door on the run. She slammed the kitchen door after him.

"She threw a pan at me," Kelso said. "She actually did. I didn't think she meant it when she said to get out."

"She meant it, all right," Dave said. "I'm glad she didn't have a gun. You raised hell and then you slid a chunk under it."

"I did for a fact," Kelso said morosely as they left the house. "You reckon she meant it when she said she never wanted to see either one of us again?"

"Sounded to me like she did," Dave answered.

Kelso sighed. "Only one thing to do. Let's go get drunk."

"Your ideas are improving," Dave said. "In fact, it's the only good idea you've had lately."

In the morning a fist pounding on Dave's door brought him awake. He staggered across the room, his head threatening to split. He opened the door a crack to see the clerk standing in the hall.

"A runner just got in from the agency," the clerk said. "The hearings start in the morning. You're supposed to get back today."

Dave groaned and slammed the door. Riding a horse would kill him, but he had it to do. He left an hour later without seeing either Sharon or Kelso.

That night Dave wrote a short letter to Sharon, telling her that he wanted to see her when he had time to go to Ouray. He assured her that he had not made any agreement with Vince to see which one would have her, that he had no idea Vince was going to come up with his idea about cutting cards to see who got her, and that he wanted her to make up her own mind.

He read the letter through again and then slipped it into

an envelope and sealed it. The letter was more formal and restrained that he wanted it to be, but under the circumstances he felt that was the way he should write.

The truth was he could not write any other way, feeling as he did toward her. He was angry and disappointed. She should have known that it was the champagne in Kelso that was talking, but even if she hadn't thought of that, she had no right to blame him for something Kelso said.

The more he thought about it, the more he was puzzled by her behavior because it did not square with the other qualities he had found in her. He felt that she was an unusually frank and honest girl with a fine sense of justice, but this was not fair, condemning him without giving him a chance to defend himself.

If she did not answer his letter, he knew it was all off between them. He would not attempt to see her again, and this hurt because he knew now he loved her and his greatest regret was his failure to tell her the night she had given him an account of her life.

The following morning the commission opened its hearings in a stable at the Los Pinos Agency. Besides the members of the commission, Major General Edward Hatch, Charles Adams, and Ouray, three other men sat at the long table: First Lieutenant Gustavus Valois of the Ninth Cavalary who served as recorder, Dave who acted as clerk, and a man named John Townsend who was hired as interpreter. Several reporters had come to the agency, but they were not admitted to the hearings, a situation which led to poor relations with the press.

The days were cold, with snow appearing on Grand Mesa and the divide between the Uncompahgre and the San Miguel. The one potbellied stove could not heat the entire room, even with a fire going full blast, for the chill air slipped around the door and through cracks in the walls.

Overhead in the loft a bunch of squirrels often rioted so loudly that they interfered with the taking of testimony. Outside a force of grim-faced Indian police under Shavano and Sapinero kept order. Inside the Utes who had come to testify before the commission were assured by General Hatch that the Milk River fight had been a fair one between the soldiers and the Indians, so none of the latter would be punished for taking part in it. This assurance opened the mouths of Jack, Colorow, and Antelope, and they gave a straightforward account of the battle which jibed with the known facts.

Hatch also said that the Indians who had murdered Nathan Meeker and the other white men at the agency and had held the three women and two children captive were to be tried and punished if found guilty. Here the commission ran into trouble. Naturally none of the White River Utes wanted to admit taking part in the massacre, so they lied about themselves and others of their tribe.

No man, white or red, would willingly incriminate himself. Dave understood this just as he understood Ouray's efforts to defend his people. The Meeker women had named twelve Indians who had taken part in the massacre and had held them prisoners, but Ouray argued against taking the testimony of women. This was strictly against Ute custom, and Dave and Adams and all of the white men who knew anything about the Utes realized that what Ouray said was true.

Ouray also argued that the White River Utes were justified in not telling the truth at the hearings because all of them were more or less involved in the massacre. He pointed out that no white man could be expected to give evidence against himself, so why should the Utes?

As the hearing wore on toward the end of November, Dave found his admiration for Ouray growing. The chief wore a white shirt, a black string necktie, and a black broadcloth suit. His hair hung down his chest in two long braids.

There were a number of days when he was too sick to attend the hearing, for Bright's disease that had been destroying his fine body was taking a greater and greater toll. But he came when he could, harnessing his fine team of blacks to his carriage and making the hour drive from his farm to the agency. There he tied his horses to a hitch rail and went into the stable. Dave, watching him, saw that on some days when his condition was worse he had to be helped to his place at the long table where he sat with the other commissioners.

He was grieving, Dave thought, because his people had been brought to this place. For twenty years he had done everything in his power to buy time for the Utes, to hold as much of their ancestral homeland as he could, but now time had run out. Dave sensed that Ouray knew this just as he knew his painracked body would not retain life much longer. Still the chief held his own with Hatch and Adams, sometimes even having the better of the exchange.

Dave often thought about the old days in the San Luis Valley when Ouray had been well and strong and his people had been free to drift from one camp to another in western Colorado whenever the notion struck them, but those days were gone and would never return. Dave wondered if dark thoughts of failure were in Ouray's mind, or was he aware he had done better than most Indian leaders in holding back the white flood? But would there be any satisfaction in the knowledge if it were in his mind?

Perhaps he thought that there was only one important fact. In the end he had failed. White man's promises written into the treaties between the United States and the Ute nation meant nothing. Now Ouray was caught in the great void between two people and their different ways of life.

Ouray wore white man's clothes and lived in a white man's house, and he had learned to harness a team and drive his carriage the way a white man would, but these skills meant nothing. He had nowhere to go these last months of his life except back to his own people, and to defeat.

This, Dave thought, must be what was in Ouray's mind. It would be in his if he were the chief. But he was Dave Rand, a white man, a citizen of a great and powerful country that was dealing with a minor tribe, a mere handful of mountain-dwelling Indians who were not guilty of all the injustices and outrages and murders that had been committed during this long struggle between the two. Now the white man's will would prevail because he was the most powerful. Ouray must have known that, too; he must

have foreseen the pattern of destiny. Still, he did not admit
defeat. He would buy as much more time for his people as
he could.

Dave did not hear from Sharon for nearly two weeks.
He had decided that she wasn't going to write and he came
close to changing his mind about riding to Ouray to see
her. Then the letter came.

My dear Dave,
I have not written because my pride has been in the
way. I have never found it easy to admit I was wrong
and to ask to be forgiven, but I have been in my own
private hell from the moment you and Vince left my
house that night. It was worse after I read your letter.
There is only one escape for me and I am taking it. I
was wrong and I am sorry I acted the way I did. I hope
you will forgive me. Please come to see me again.

Most sincerely,
Sharon

Dave read the letter three times before he slipped it back
into the envelope. Life with Sharon would never be dull,
he thought. He wrote a short note saying that he would
come to Ouray to see her as soon as he could, that the
hearings were dragging out and he didn't know when he
could get away.

Two things happened that relieved the monotony of the
hearings. First, Agent Stanley who had been on a drunk
was removed by Secretary Schurz. The second had more
bearing on the hearings. Charles Adams introduced the
testimony he had taken at Greeley from the Meeker women
and Mrs. Price in which they all had sworn they had been
raped by the Indians during the time they were held as
prisoners.

Raping women captives was no crime from the Ute
point of view. On the contrary, in their eyes it would have
been strange if it had not been done, so bringing this out
and having it recorded by Lieutenant Valois did not worry
the average Ute who sat on the floor in the stable and
listened to what was being said, but Ouray understood

what it meant to white people and how it would affect public opinion.

When Ouray left the hearing, he told Dave that by white man's standards it was all right for a white man to rape a Ute woman, but if a Ute raped a white woman, it was a crime which was not to be overlooked or forgiven. He turned and walked slowly to his carriage, untied his team, and painfully pulled himself into the seat.

Dave watched him drive away, telling himself that either the women had lied on Grand Mesa when they had been rescued, or they had lied to Adams when they had given him their statement in Greeley. If they had lied on Grand Mesa, it must have been to save their reputation. If they had lied in Greeley, it probably was because they were afraid the murderers of their husband and father would escape being punished. They knew that the knowledge they had been outraged would stir public opinion against the Utes as nothing else would.

Both explanations were understandable, Dave thought, and the truth would more than likely never been known, but he doubted that Ouray understood. Even if he did, he would never agree that the testimony of a woman should be given credence in the hearings, but Adams had insisted on introducing the women's testimony just the same. They had named twelve Utes who had taken part in the massacre and had abused them when they were held captive. These were the men who were to be tried.

Ouray did not return to the hearings for several days. He sent word that he was sick, and Dave, remembering how slowly he had walked to his carriage and how painfully he had pulled himself into the seat, believed that it was so.

When he returned at last, he did not drive his carriage with his fine team of blacks, but rode a buckskin horse. He had no hat, his black hair was shiny with grease and smoothed flat against his head. He had left his broadcloth suit at home. In its place he wore a buckskin outfit with beautiful beadwork. When he entered the stable, he did not take his place with the other commissioners at the long table, but walked to the other end of the room and sat on the floor in the circle made by the Ute men. He had returned to his people as Dave had known he must.

Jack testified that day, and again the following day. Ouray did not return the third morning. Snow was on the ground when the hearings opened on the fourth day. It was well into December, and Dave sensed that the hearings had dragged on as long as anyone could stand them. Now it was time to finish. Ouray was there along with Colorow and Jack and a number of men of the White River band. A few Uncompahgres including Shavano and Sapinero had come into the stable.

There was no more testimony to be taken, so Adams talked, reciting what had happened and demanding that the twelve men named by the Meeker women be given up for trial. Adams told the Indians that if they refused to produce the accused men, the soldiers would come and hunt them down, and pointed out that the Utes could not afford a war with a nation that had forty million people.

Then Ouray spoke with great dignity and feeling, telling the whites that any talk about going to war was foolish, that he had said it many times and all of the Utes understood how foolish it would be. The other Indians talked after Ouray finished, then General Hatch rose and slammed his hands down hard upon the table and spoke sharply, saying that only Chief Douglas and Johnson of the White River Utes had come in. He read the full list again and said that they must be turned over for trial, that it was up to the Indians to comply.

Ouray translated what he had said. After that there was silence. It seemed to Dave that this was the climax of the hearings, that even as he sat at the table the circle of Indians was drawn tighter. None of them so much as glanced at the white men, none of them moved, and for a time there was no sound but the snapping of the fire in the potbellied stove and the scurrying of the squirrels in the loft above them.

Dave did not look at Adams or Hatch or Valois. He was staring at the Indian circle the way a man would stare at the beady eyes of a rattlesnake that was within striking distance. The chilly prickles raced up and down his spine again. He had felt those prickles that day on Grand Mesa when he'd sat in Douglas's lodge with Adams and Leslie, knowing that he was very close to death. He had not felt them during the hearings until now.

Suddenly Dave thought of facts that had not seemed very important when Ouray was dressed in his broadcloth suit and rode to the hearings in his carriage behind the team of blacks. Now the climate had changed. Ouray was sitting in the Indian circle. His gaze, along with Jack's and Shavano's and the others, was fixed on the floor in the center of the ring.

Dave wondered if Ouray was thinking of the same facts he was, that there were not more than twenty-five white men around the agency, including only fourteen soldiers, but there must be hundreds of Indians, fifty at least in the police force which had been organized to keep order and was never far from the stable. Inside the stable at the other end of the long room from the handful of white men at the table were fifteen or more Indians.

The room was not warm, but sweat dribbled down Dave's face to gather in tiny globules on his chin and from there drop to the table. He told himself that it was foolish to think that these Indians would attack the white men at the table. Or was it? They were led by Ouray and Shavano and Sapinero, men who knew that only a savage punishment waited for them if they murdered the white men who were in this room. But Indians were as unpredictable as children, and such a murder was not without precedent. Dave was remembering the killing of General Edward Canby during a conference with Captain Jack and his Modoes in northern California back in 1873.

Suddenly the great mountain of flesh that was Colorow moved. He threw his knife violently into the center of the Indian ring where the blade struck the splintery floor and stuck there. Dave half-rose from his chair and fell back. If he or the other whites in the room made a wrong move, or showed the fear that must be in all of them, a blood bath would follow like the one at the White River Agency. Then Colorow drew his stone pipe from inside his shirt and laid it beside the knife.

Slowly every man in the circle drew his knife and laid it in the center, and then the pipes went down beside the knives. This was the choice, Dave knew; after all the haggling and the taking of testimony, this was the moment of decision, of life or death for the white men who sat here, and eventually the life or death of the Ute nation.

The knife meant war, the pipe peace. Now, in this smelly stable the immediate destiny that waited for Dave Rand would not be decided by Secretary Schurz or General Sherman or President Hayes, but by a few mountain-dwelling, freedom-loving Utes who might very well choose death rather than removal from their beloved ancestral homeland, the valleys of the Grand and the Uncompahgre and Thigunawat where dwelt the spirits of their departed ones.

None of the men at the table moved. There was not even the sound of breathing. And then, for some strange reason, the thought came to Dave that if they died here in this stable, Sharon would hear about it and she would say it was exactly what she expected. What else could anyone expect from the red-skinned monsters who had killed her uncle?

Then, as suddenly as Colorow had thrown the knife, Ouray rose and walked toward the table. He said, "You want our answer. Now you will have it."

He paused. Dave took a long breath as the weakness of relief flooded his body. There would be no murders here, he thought. At least not today.

"You want our land," Ouray went on. "You have taken it piece by piece, and now you want what is left. We will not leave it. We will fight. Your soldiers will come and will die in our mountains."

He turned his black eyes to Adams. "You were my friend but now are my enemy." He looked at Hatch. "You are my enemy. I cannot expect justice from any of you. Adams is a Colorado man and all Colorado men are our enemies. We will not let the twelve men you are asking for be tried in a Colorado court where they will not get justice. We will give these men up only if they are tried in Washington where I have at least one friend."

He walked back to the Indian circle and sat down on the floor with the others. General Hatch said, "I have already asked your friend, Secretary Schurz, to give you and some other chiefs permission to go to Washington and testify. I will send another message telling him of your request."

The Indians talked among themselves and presently two of them walked out of the stable. Ouray said, "Jack and Colorow have left to bring the men you want, but we will not give them to you until we hear what Secretary Schurz decides."

General Hatch adjourned the hearings until the commissioners heard from Schurz. On December 11 a telegram came from Schurz giving permission to try the twelve Utes outside of Colorado. Dave stayed at the agency long enough to complete his report to the Secretary, then left for Ouray.

9

Dave had not forgotten about Major Leslie telling him that
Clyde Nelson was working for the agency herding cattle. He
had hoped that Nelson would ride in from the cow camp,
but he never did. When a jag of cattle was brought to the
agency to feed the Indians, it was always some of the other
cow hands who drove them. But now, on his way to
Ouray, Dave decided he had time to ride up Cow Creek
and talk to Nelson.

He had no trouble finding the camp. He dismounted at
the cabin, noting that several riders were easing the cattle
through the thin covering of snow down the creek toward
the river. Another man was cutting wood among the piñons
and cedars on the side of the hill above the camp.

From where Dave stood beside the cabin, he studied the
riders and decided none of them was Nelson. He climbed
the hill and approached the woodcutter from the back.
When he was within a few feet of him he saw that it was
Nelson, although the years had changed him, turning his
hair white and making him stoop-shouldered.

Dave said, "Howdy, Clyde."

Nelson whirled and peered at Dave, then he said, "It's
Dave Rand, ain't it? You've growed up some since I seen
you."

Dave held out his hand, shocked when he saw how
much Nelson had aged. He wasn't over fifty, but his faded
blue eyes and the deep lines in his face gave him an
old-man look.

Nelson shook hands and pulled back immediately, acting as if he wished Dave had not appeared out of the past

to stir old memories he wanted to forget. Dave said, "I guess I have growed some since then. Been quite a while."

Nelson took his hat off his head and ran a hand through his shaggy white hair. "Yeah, quite a while."

"Sam Leslie told me you were here," Dave said.

"He got me this job," Nelson said. "He's a good man."

"I've been at the agency," Dave said. "I thought you'd bring the cattle in some time."

"The other boys do the herding." Nelson stared down the valley to where Cow Creek emptied into the Uncompahgre. "I do the cooking and rustle the wood and such." He felt in his pocket for his pipe and tobacco and drew them out. "We got this skiff of snow on the ground and chances are we'll get more, so we've got to drive the herd down the valley a piece where they'll find grass."

Silence then, and Dave realized that he and Clyde Nelson had nothing to talk about. It would be a mistake to mention Mrs. Nelson or Arvado. He was talking to a shadow. When he thought of the man Clyde Nelson had been, strong and independent and resourceful, he had all he could do to keep from crying. The drunk who had murdered Arvado might as well have gunned Clyde Nelson down, too, for he had killed him just as certainly as if he had shot him.

Dave wondered why Sam Leslie had said Clyde would want to see him. Perhaps he thought that Dave's appearance would do the man some good, but it hadn't. Nelson just stood there absently staring into space and wanting Dave to leave.

"I've got to get moving," Dave said. "I was going to Ouray and thought I'd stop by and say howdy."

"Glad you did," Nelson mumbled.

"So long," Dave said.

Dave walked down the hill to his horse and stepped into the saddle. As he rode away he heard the steady *chunk-chunk* of Nelson's ax as it bit into the trunk of the piñon tree he was cutting down.

When he reached Ouray, Dave was in no mood to see Sharon, so he took a hotel room and had supper in the dining room. He felt better then, although he still had a feeling he was haunted by the ghost of the Clyde Nelson he had known years ago, and as he walked along the snow-packed street to Sharon's house, he considered how one tragedy spread to touch other lives. Clyde and his wife had loved Arvado as a son. Even if Mrs. Nelson had lived, she would probably have been destroyed in spirit just as Clyde had been.

The front of Sharon's house was dark, but when he knocked, she came out of her kitchen, set the lamp on the cutting table and opened the door. Dave said, ''I'm here.''

''Dave.''

She made his name a sound of joy. She took his hands and pulled him into the room seemingly unaware of the cold air that flowed through the open door. She hugged him, her head against his chest, and then he realized she was crying.

''Wait a minute,'' he said. ''What are the tears for?''

She drew back and looked at him, the tears glistening on her cheeks. She tried to say something and swallowed and then she blurted, ''I was such a fool, Dave. I thought I had lost you and I love you so much.''

''I've thought the same,'' he said. ''I love you, too. Will you marry me?''

''Oh yes, Dave,'' she said. ''I'll marry you tonight or tomorrow or any day you say.''

He pulled her to him and kissed her, and when he let her go, he said, ''Honey, that's a kiss I'll never forget as long as I live.''

She shut the door and, picking up the lamp, took his hand and led him into the kitchen. She said, ''I've been expecting you. I baked a cake today and I'll heat the coffee up. If you haven't had supper, I'll fix something.''

''Just the cake,'' he said. ''I got in kind of late and ate in the hotel.''

She backed away, her arms hugging her breasts, her gaze on him as if she could not see enough of him. She said slowly, ''I told you I'd marry you, but you'd better remember that sometimes I do the worst things. I've got a terrible temper, and even when I don't want to let it get away from me, it does. I'm prejudiced against the Indians and I don't think I can change. I don't want to go back East with you. I couldn't live there. I'm just a mess, darling, and if you want to reconsider . . ."

He laughed. "I've considered this carefully and I'll still take you. Bring on the cake."

"Right away." As she cut the cake and lifted the slices to the serving plates, she said, "Tell me about the hearings. I've been reading the *Solid Muldoon* and I judge its editor and star reporter Dave Day got a little cold."

"He sure did," Dave said, smiling. "When his whisky ran out, he got pretty unhappy. I expect he came back to Ouray and got warmed up in the first saloon he could find."

He told her briefly what had happened while she built the fire up and warmed the coffee. As she filled the cup in front of him, she said, "The Meeker women were outraged, weren't they?"

He did not doubt his love for her, and yet it was strange how she could stir his anger so quickly with such a question. It was her tone of voice, he thought, more than the actual words she used.

He waited until his temper was controlled, then he said, "They changed their story, so we don't know for sure. Now about this business of going back East, Sharon. I don't want to go, either. I guess I'd better tell you about myself or you'll be buying a pig in a poke."

"I'll take this pig in any old poke he comes in," she said, laughing, "but go ahead and inflict the story of your life on me just the way I did on you."

He told her about his first memories of Kansas, his life in Denver, then the move to the San Luis Valley and the murder of his mother and Alonzo Freeman. He finished with an account of his schooling in Denver, his apprenticeship with the *Daily News*, his drifting years and finally meeting Carl Schurz and taking the assignment that had brought him back to Colorado.

"I guess I should apologize for not telling you all the truth," he said, "but no one except Major Leslie and

Charles Adams were supposed to know the real reason for me being here.''

"Well then," she said as if a mystery had suddenly become clear, "I see why you feel you have to defend the Utes. If you're working for Carl Schurz, you naturally have to take that side.''

Everybody, he guessed, had a blind spot, and Sharon's was the Ute Indians. He saw no use in going over the same ground again. She did not want to understand, so she wouldn't. It was a subject which must be avoided as long as they were in Ute country, but once they were away, it would not have the meaning that it had now.

"I'll be in Colorado a few more days," he said. "Maybe a few weeks. I have to report to the Secretary until everything at the agency is wrapped up. It won't be long. After that I have to go to the Southern Ute Agency and then to the San Carlos Agency in Arizona. I don't know where I'll go from there, but before I'm done, I guess I'll see about every agency in Arizona and New Mexico. We'll get married as soon as I get back. It'll be up to you to set the date.''

"I'd set it tomorrow if you leave it up to me," she said quickly, and both of them laughed. "Why can't I go with you?''

"Department regulations, I guess," he said. "Mostly because it's too dangerous for a woman, and accommodations at some of the agencies are awful.''

"You don't have to go," she protested. "You can resign.''

He shook his head. "I gave my word, but as soon as I do what I agreed to, I will resign. I've been thinking I'd like to buy a newspaper in some small town out here. All I know is that I belong in the West. The years I spent back East gave me a sort of education, so I don't begrudge them, but I belong out here. I was reminded of that on the train coming into Canon City. I had a funny feeling that I'd come home even though I hadn't lived here for years.''

"It seems a long time ago," she said softly. "So much has happened.''

For an hour or more they sat on the divan, his arm around her, her head on his shoulder, and planned their future. When he said it was time he went back to the hotel, she said, "Tell me again you love me and tell me why."

"I love you," he said. "I'll tell you why."

"All right, tell me, you idiot," she said, her mouth against his shirt so her words were muffled. "I've done so many stupid things since you met me that I don't know why you love me."

"I love you because you're beautiful," he said, "and you're a good cook and you have a good figure with curves and everything."

"Figure!" She sniffed. "A lot you can tell with all the clothes a woman has to wear."

"I know it's good beneath all those clothes," he said. "I've got faith."

She raised her head to look at him sternly. "You've been undressing me in your mind."

"Certainly."

"Oh, you are an idiot." She laughed and kissed him, and then said seriously, "I don't think you've given me the real reason."

"All right," he said, "let's try this one. I love you because you're the first honest woman I ever met. You tell me your faults, but the women I knew in Washington pretended they had angel wings and were without blemish."

"They were liars," she said, pleased.

"Now you can tell me why you love me," he said.

She was holding his hand that was next to hers. Now she raised it to her lips and kissed it and then rose and walked across the room. She said, standing with her back to him, "I don't know, Dave, I really don't. I've quarreled with you. I've been so mad at you I thought I hated you. I've done silly, stupid things like telling you to get out and saying I didn't want to ever see you again when all the time I knew I didn't mean it and I knew that if I lost you, I didn't want to live."

She whirled to face him, her skirt flaring away from her trim ankles. "I've got such a perverse disposition, Dave, but I never acted this way before I met you. I've met other men I liked. For instance, I liked Vince and I think I could marry him and be reasonably happy, but I would never love him. That's why I was so angry that night when I thought you two had talked me over and cold-bloodedly decided you'd cut the cards to see who was going to marry me. If he'd been here alone, I wouldn't have lost my temper, but I just couldn't stand the thought that you were taking me for granted in a lukewarm kind of way.''

He rose and went to her. ''I was mad, too, you see, because I thought you were being unfair. That was why my letter was kind of formal.''

''I understand that,'' she said, ''and I hope you understand why I was so slow to write to you. It was the hardest thing I ever had to do.''

She bit her lip as if undecided whether she should say what she had in mind, and then she hurried on. ''Dave, don't laugh at me, but that evening when the train pulled into Canon City and you came up behind me and asked if you could help with my luggage, I looked over my shoulder at you and I had the craziest feeling.

''It seemed that a bunch of bells had started to ring and fireworks were exploding and all the things you read about in novels were happening. I'd never looked at a man before and had anything like that happen. That was why I decided to come on to Ouray even when I was scared of the Indians. I just wanted to be with you and give you a chance to like me.''

''It worked,'' he said. ''It worked just fine.''

Later when he walked back to the hotel, he admitted to himself that he had no idea why he had fallen in love with Sharon. Not that it made any difference. A man was the worst kind of a fool to try to determine why he was in love. All he knew was that it had happened and he was glad of it.

The next day Dave discovered that it was impossible to buy a diamond engagement ring in Ouray. He told Sharon that night, and although he saw that she was disappointed, there was nothing he could do about it.

"We can get married here when I get back," he said, "or we can wait until we get to Denver and have our honeymoon there. Either way you will have both an engagement and a wedding ring. I promise."

"I know I will, honey," she said. "I'm not blaming you. It's the price I pay for living in this stupid little wilderness town. I don't know where you'll buy your newspaper, or where we'll live, but please don't let it be Ouray."

"It won't," he said. "I promise that, too. I wouldn't try to compete with Dave Day and his *Solid Muldoon*."

When he told her good-bye that night, he said, "I have to get back to the agency in the morning. I may not see you for quite a while. You won't have a ring to wear, so you'll just have to tell the men you're taken, Vince especially."

"I'll tell him," she promised.

When Dave returned to the agency, he found that Charles Adams had left for Manitou Springs. General Hatch complained that the twelve wanted Utes had disappeared. A new agent had arrived, a man in his early fifties named Ben Harlan who had once served at the agency as an interpreter. He was a quiet, slow-moving man who had great respect for the rights of the Indians. Once in Dave's hearing he remarked that his job was to protect the Utes, not the whites.

This seemed to Dave an extreme position for an Indian agent to take, yet there was some grounds for him taking it. The newspapers of the state still shouted, "The Utes must go." Governor Pitkin had not changed his attitude, and, back in Washington, Senator Teller prepared to make an attack on Carl Schurz because of the Department's Indian policy.

Dave remained at the agency for the rest of the meetings which had to do with making plans for the hearings that would be held in Washington and for the surrender of the twelve Utes that the government wanted to try. The latter presented a problem. Not only had the twelve Utes disappeared, but the Indians seemed reluctant to give them up.

Although Ouray made two trips to the camp of the White River Utes, he was unable to bring in the wanted men.

Late in December, Dave accompanied the other white members of the commission to Major Leslie's place where they were to meet Ouray and the rest of the Utes who were to go to Washington, but when the Indians arrived, none of the twelve Utes were with them.

General Hatch was furious. He talked to Dave and Ouray about returning to Los Pinos and hunting for the fugitives until they were captured. Dave advised against it, with winter at hand. The high country always had a heavy snowfall, and it was doubtful that the Uncompahgres would help track down the wanted men.

Ouray said it would be foolish, that to the best of his knowledge, the fugitives were on a hunting trip in Utah somewhere around the La Sal Mountains, and even if Hatch had a large force it would be impossible to find the wanted men in that wilderness of deep canyons and mountains and mesas that to the white men was still unexplored.

There was nothing for Hatch to do but move the Washington-bound Indians in mule-pulled wagons through the snow to Alamosa where they boarded the narrowgauge for the East. Dave remained at Leslie's ranch long enough to buy the bay gelding he had been riding since the major had loaned him the horse in October.

He returned to the agency where he wrote out his final report, making a strong recommendation that troops be moved to the reservation as soon as the weather permitted. The Indians must be protected against the whites. The more he thought about the agent's remark, the more he realized it was true that the Utes needed protection. The white had anticipated moving onto the reservation for months, and now thousands of settlers and prospectors were ready to jump across the line the instant they thought they would be reasonably safe.

The soldiers should be used to hold the whites off the reservation, Dave argued, or the invaders would cross the line illegally. Some would surely be murdered by the Indians, and incidents of that nature would make the final

solution more difficult than ever, or possibly even bring on
another blood bath that had been so narrowly averted on
more than one occasion after the Milk Creek battle and the
Meeker massacre.

As he addressed and stamped a large envelope and
slipped the bulky report into it, he wondered what Ouray
thought he could accomplish in Washington when he talked
with Secretary Schurz. The deck was stacked against the
chief, Dave thought sadly. Ouray was gallant and brave
and intelligent, but the odds of forty million whites against
a few thousand Utes made only one decision possible.
Ouray had bought time for his people, but he would not be
able to avert final defeat. The question in Dave's mind was
whether the chief would live long enough to see the final
decision made.

The next morning, the last day of the year, Dave left for
Ouray. He found that Vince Kelso had just pulled in with a
load of Duke Conway's freight. The two men had fought
snowdrifts in the mountains that would have defeated the
average freighter, but not Duke Conway. Although Kelso
was exhausted, he insisted on waiting out the old year with
Sharon and Dave and seeing the new one in.

This time Dave bought the champagne. When Dave told
Kelso that Sharon had promised to marry him, he stared at
his glass for a long moment before he could lift his head to
meet Dave's gaze. He said slowly, "I guess I always
thought that by some kind of strange miracle, I'd win, but
I didn't." He raised his glass to Sharon and bowed.
"Here's to your happiness. May you have lots of troubles and
all of them little ones."

Sharon flushed and said, "Thank you, Vince, but please
don't wish me too many."

Kelso left a few minutes later. Dave stayed until after
midnight when a great racket all up and down Main Street
indicated that the infant year of 1880 had been safely
ushered in. Dave said, "I've got to leave for the Southern
Ute Agency in the morning, so I guess I'd better go to
bed."

But she could not let him go for a little while. She put
her hands around his neck and lifted her face for his kiss.

Then she drew back and whispered, "I would beg you not to go and to resign your job if I thought it would do any good, but you are the strongest man I ever met. I don't mean physically, your strength is inside you. I'll have to get used to living with that kind of strength because I never saw it in my home. Neither Dad nor Uncle Ben had it." She swallowed, and added, "Please come back to me, Dave. I need you very much."

"I'll come back," he said. "You see, I need you, too."

When he reached the hotel, he found Kelso waiting for him. He said, "I'll buy you a drink, Dave."

"Sounds good," Dave said. "It's the last drink we'll have together for a while. I'm leaving in the morning. I'll expect you to look after Sharon while I'm gone."

Surprised, Kelso asked, "You trust me, all the time knowing I'll have a hell of a time keeping my hands off her?"

"I trust you," Dave said, "but I trust her more than I do you."

They crossed the lobby to the bar. Kelso ordered whisky for both of them. When he lifted his glass, his lips were flat against his teeth, his eyes narrowed and wicked. He said, "You're a fool, leaving her this way. I hope you break your damned neck while you're gone. I'll have her if you do."

"I aim to look out for my neck," Dave said, "and you'd better get one thing straight. If you lay a hand on her while I'm gone, I'll break your neck."

"That's plain enough," Kelso put his glass down, the liquor untasted. "You'd have a right, too. You're a good man, Dave, and you'll make her a good husband. I'm supposed to say something about the best man winning and you'd better make her happy and all that, but I can't think of nothing to say except that I want to be the man to do it."

Dave lifted his glass and drank, not knowing what to say. He had not known, either, how much Kelso loved Sharon. He had never taken his rival seriously because he'd always had a feeling that Kelso was the kind of man who habitually chased women and let them go the minute he captured them.

Dave set his glass back on the cherrywood bar as he said, "I'll see you when I get back, Vince. Thanks for the drink."

He went upstairs to his room, leaving Kelso staring moodily at his glass of whisky. Dave was more troubled about leaving then he had thought he would be. He had told Sharon he'd probably be gone six months. That was too long, he thought. Too much could happen in that time, especially between a woman as beautiful and passionate as Sharon and a man as much in love with her as Vince Kelso.

10

The six months that Dave had expected to spend working for the Department of the Interior turned into seven and then eight. He was well into the ninth when he wrote out his last report to Carl Schurz and mailed it in Santa Fe. He rode out of town the following morning at sunup.

Dave had read the newspapers and had had enough correspondence with Carl Schurz to know what had happened to the Utes. In Pueblo the party bound for Washington had been met by a mob of hoodlums that had thrown rocks and pieces of coal at the Indians. Apparently it had been touch and go for a time because the authorities had not anticipated anything like that happening and had not provided adequate protection. If the twelve wanted men had been in the party, the chances were they would have been lynched.

The only White River Ute who had suffered any punishment was Douglas. He was imprisoned without a trial at Fort Leavenworth and was still there. In Washington, the hearings before the House Committee on Indian Affairs dragged out until March 22. Little was learned that had not been brought out in the hearings in the smelly stable at the Los Pinos Agency, but Ouray and Carl Schurz did work out an agreement.

The bargain was not a good one for the Utes. Dave, reading about it in the newspapers, knew that it must have gone against Ouray's grain, but the chief was as aware as anyone of the pressure that was being brought to bear by both the politicians and the Colorado newspapers; he knew exactly how Governor Pitkin and Senator Teller felt, so he had made the best deal he could.

The agreement provided that the White River Utes were to be moved to Utah where they would occupy part of the Uintah reservation. The Southern Utes were to remain in the state, but their land would be cut in size by one-third. The Uncompahgres were to be given agricultural land near the junction of the Grand and the Gunnison, if enough land could be found there. Individual allotments were to be made, a plan that was called "lands in severalty."

Early in April, Ouray and the rest of the Utes who had been in Washington returned to Los Pinos, and Senator Teller made a virulent attack upon Secretary Schurz on the floor of the Senate. He said that communal landholdings had always been the Indian custom, not individual holdings, and that the Indian should be treated as a savage and not a civilized man. He scorned the notion that the Utes who had signed the agreement had any idea what holding "lands in severalty" meant.

In spite of the senator's attack, Schurz remained in office, and Dave was confident that he would continue as Secretary of the Interior as long as Rutherford B. Hayes was in the White House.

Ouray who had suffered from Bright's disease for so long died on August 24 while visiting the Southern Utes. He had gone there hoping to help persuade his fellow tribesmen to sign the agreement. When Dave read about Ouray's death, he wondered how the chief could have stood the long ride from Los Pinos to the Southern Ute Agency, and if he had suspected when he had left the Uncompahgre with Chipeta and a few friends that this would be the last trip he would ever make.

Dave rode north, getting his meals when he could and sleeping wherever darkness overtook him. He kept his bay gelding at as fast a pace as he dared. Suddenly the time since he had left Sharon seemed like centuries.

As long as he had been busy it had not been so bad, but now that he had resigned and was actually on his way to see Sharon, he could not get the miles behind him fast enough. He had to pull his horse down time after time, realizing he could kill the animal if he kept him at that pace. Sometimes he dismounted and trotted alongside the bay; every night he saw to it that the animal was well fed and watered and rubbed down.

He had written often to Sharon and he had heard from her, although not as regularly as he wrote to her. He was on the move so much that letters often arrived at an agency after he left. Sometimes they piled up and he would receive three or four at one time. He had hoped this would happen at Sante Fe, but it hadn't, and when he left, he was unable to rid himself of a burden of anxiety. He had not heard from her for more than a month.

Sharon's last letter held a note of discontent that bothered Dave. During the summer people had moved in and new mines had opened up, and she admitted that Ouray was a different camp than it had been when she arrived nearly a year ago. Still, she had come to hate it and she asked Dave to hurry. She wanted a permanent home of her own, she could not stand the lonely life she was living.

She seldom mentioned Vince Kelso. This, too, worried Dave. He trusted her, and yet the devil of doubt lingered in his mind. He could not forget Kelso's words, ''I hope you break your damned neck while you're gone. I'll have her if you do.''

Well, he hadn't broken his neck, but he had been gone a long time, and he knew from Sharon's letters that these extra months had been hard to bear. He would not have worried if he could have gone to her early in July as he had planned, but now it was late September, with the scrub oak turned scarlet and the quakies making yellow and orange strips through the spruce. Fresh snow was on the peaks, and the chilly nights were ominous with the threat of an early winter.

He had been gone almost three months longer than he had said. He could not blame Sharon if she had broken her promise and married Kelso or some other man she had met after Dave left, but he could not stand it if she had.

When he reached Ouray he rode directly to Sharon's house, knowing that he needed a shave and had the gamy smell of a man who has made a long, hard ride without changing clothes or taking a bath, but the suspense had tightened his nerves with each mile until he had to know.

He knocked, but he did not hear anyone coming to the door. He shivered, for the sun was nearly down and the breeze that had been cooled by the high peaks which surrounded Ouray was sharp and penetrating.

He knocked again, so hard this time that the door rattled under his fist. He wondered what he would do if Vince answered his knock and told him he was too late, that he and Sharon were married. His heart began to pound. No, he couldn't stand it, he told himself. If that happened, he'd kill Kelso.

He raised his fist to knock again when he heard someone cross the room. An audible sigh broke out of him. Maybe she'd been asleep. In any case she was here. The footsteps were not those of a man.

The knob turned and the door opened slowly. Stunned, Dave stared at the middle-aged woman who stood there. She was a stranger to him, tall and angular, possessing neither grace nor beauty. Her lips curled in scorn as she stared at him. She said, "You've come to the wrong house. The girls you're looking for are yonder." She jerked a thumb toward the next block. "I'm a good woman and don't you mistake me for a . . ."

"Where's Sharon Morgan?" he shouted.

"Don't you yell at me," she said angrily.

She started to shut the door in his face, but he shoved a booted foot forward between the door and the casing. He said evenly, "I apologize for shouting at you. Now will you please tell me where Sharon is?"

She scowled, then said in a civil tone, "You must be her feeonsay. Rand. Dave Rand. That's your name, ain't it?"

He had waited too long to dilly-dally like this. He grabbed her arms and shook her. "Damn it, will you tell me where she is?"

She drove her heel down sharply on the instep of his right foot, a savage blow that hurt and brought an involuntary exclamation of pain from him. She jerked free and stepped back.

"I never seen a man I couldn't handle in one way or another," she said tartly. "Now I'll tell you something. Cussing and manhandling me ain't gonna get you nowhere."

He leaned against the door casing staring at the woman, as nearly out of his mind as he had ever been in his life. He waited a moment until the red spots that had been rushing across his eyes cleared away, then he said slowly, "Just tell me where she is and I won't bother you any more. Is she here?"

"No." The woman hesitated, looking down her long nose at him as if wondering whether he was worth helping. Finally she said, "I've got a letter for you. She left on the stage this morning."

The woman turned and stalked across the room and into the kitchen. Sharon had left this morning! He had missed her by a matter of hours. He still didn't know if she was married. If she was . . . But there was no sense in thinking of that possibility. She wasn't. She couldn't be.

The woman came back, an envelope in her hand. She said, "Sharon is a nice girl. She told me you were a fine man, but she could have done a lot better."

Dave jerked the envelope out of her hand and turned away. The woman cried, "Why, you're the most ungrateful whelp I ever seen."

He stepped into the saddle and rode away, not wanting the woman to see him read the letter. For some reason he expected the worst. Otherwise she wouldn't have left, giving his letter to that woman. It was the only connecting link he had with Sharon. He might have missed it entirely, the woman being the kind of creature that she was.

As soon as he turned the corner he tore the envelope open and took out a single sheet of paper, his hand shaking.

Darling,

I know you'll be here any day, but I don't know which day and I just can't stay any longer, so I'm taking the stage in the morning. I had a good chance to sell the shop and I didn't want to lose the deal, so I'm moving out. I'll stay in the Windsor Hotel in Denver and I'll expect to see you there. I hope it will be soon. I miss you so much.

With all my love,
Sharon

He slipped the sheet of paper back into the envelope, a feeling in him that was almost a sickness. It was, he guessed, the kind of feeling that a condemned man has who is close to execution and unexpectedly receives a reprieve. It was going to be all right. If he left early in the morning he would reach Leslie's place tomorrow and get on past it several miles. He would catch her, probably at Cleora.

The following morning he stopped at the agency for dinner, hoping to see the agent, Ben Harlan, but one of the agency employees told him the agent had left for Leslie's ranch. "Some kind of trouble there," the man said worriedly. "None of us here know whether to stay or run. When you think about what happened to Meeker last year . . ."

"What kind of trouble?" Dave demanded.

"I don't rightly know," the man said, "except that it was something about Shavano's son Johnson being murdered by a white man. Mr. Harlan was gonna go to the Army post from here and get some soldiers. It's us I'm worried about. The Injuns have been feeling mean . . ."

Dave didn't listen. He wheeled and stepped into the saddle and rode on, fear squeezing his chest so tightly it was hard to breathe. The possibility of an Indian war was not to be discounted, now that Ouray was gone. Sharon, who hated and feared the Indians, might not have gone through to Gunnison. The chances were good that Major Leslie had held the stage up at his ranch. If that was true, she would be safe, but if the stage had gone on, and the Uncompahgres had risen as the White River Utes had a year ago . . .

But he could not bring himself to think of that. She would not be able to go through what the Meeker women and Mrs. Price had. If she had been faced with such an ordeal, she would be dead by now.

Dave followed the river for an hour or more after he left the agency. He swung away from the river, angling toward Cedar Creek. He topped Cerro and started down the long grade to the Cimarron. The sun had set and the light was so thin when he reached Sam Leslie's place that he did not see the stagecoach in the yard until he reined toward the stable. He was sure then that the trouble was bad and Leslie had held the eastbound stage. If it was that way, Sharon would be here.

As he dismounted two men came along the runway of the stable. When they stepped into the cone of down-thrown light from the lantern hanging above the door, Dave saw that one was Sam Leslie, the other Mike Collins, one of Leslie's cow hands who had worked here when Dave had waited to see Leslie nearly a year ago.

Dave stepped forward, his hand extended. "I'm glad to see you, Major."

"Dave," Leslie shouted as if he didn't believe what he saw. "Miss Morgan said you might be along, but I sure wasn't looking for you."

"She's here?"

"She's here, all right," Leslie said. "She's been telling me all day that you'll settle this business as soon as you get here."

Dave shook hands with Collins, asking, "How are you, Mike?"

The cowboy grinned. "I'm scared, Dave. I reckon I'm about as scared as I ever was in my life."

Dave turned back to Leslie. "I want to see Sharon as bad as she wants to see me. Maybe more, but I guess I'd better find out what happened first."

"You don't know?" Leslie asked, surprised. "I thought that was what fetched you."

"No, I didn't get done with my job as soon as I thought I would," Dave said. "I rode into Ouray last night and found out that Sharon had taken the stage yesterday morning. I left Ouray early today and stopped at the agency long enough to find out that young Johnson had been murdered. I came on without any dinner, so I'm hungry."

"Take care of his horse, Mike," Leslie said. "Come into the house with me. I'll have Mrs. Patrick fix you something to eat and you can talk to Miss Morgan while it's cooking. She's probably in her room. She's as scared as anybody, but I never saw a woman who had more faith in her man. If you pull a miracle out of your hat, I'll turn this whole thing over to you."

They started toward the house, Dave asking, "Well, what did happen?"

"There's two stories and they don't jibe a little bit," Leslie said. "If we knew for sure which one was true, we'd know better what to do. A couple of Ute boys, Johnson and Young Bucks, had been hunting somewhere on the Little Blue. They started home about dawn this morning when they saw a freight outfit and a cook fire. They hadn't had any luck and they were hungry, so they rode into the freighters' camp. Johnson asked for something to eat. Up to here the stories hang together, but from now on they don't.

"According to the white men, the boys were drunk. When the freighters wouldn't feed them, they got abusive. Johnson jacked a shell into the chamber of his rifle and threatened them, then the boys rode off. They hadn't gone very far till Johnson looked back. One of the freighters said he was going to shoot, so he fired first. He claims he didn't know he'd hit Johnson very hard, but he got worried, and decided they'd better come here where they'd be safe. They got here mighty early, so I'm guessing they knew, all right. When they told me about it, I held them here and sent word to Ben Harlan. I knew there'd be hell to pay with Ouray dead and the Utes feeling ornery the way they've been. I held the stage, too, figuring it would be a sitting duck for the Indians if they decided to take a few scalps. If it had been anybody but Shavano's son, it wouldn't be so bad."

They had reached the front of the house and stopped, Leslie taking out his pipe and filling it. Dave asked, "What's the Ute story?"

"It's just Young Bucks' word and he's bound to be as prejudiced on his side as the freighters are on theirs. Johnson's dead. We know that for sure. Ben Harlan saw the body. He said the boy was shot in the side below the ribs. The bullet angled up into his lungs. He couldn't have lived more than a few minutes, but he probably stayed on his horse long enough to get out of sight."

"Did Young Bucks say that Johnson was going to shoot?"

"He says no. He claims this freighter had been holding a gun on them. When they rode off they were scared he was going to cut loose. He says Johnson looked back to see what the freighter was doing and just as he turned, the man fired. If this is true, it's cold-blooded murder. Of course that's what the Indians say it is and they're demanding that I hand the freighter over to them. They'll kill him, of course."

"And if you don't?"

Leslie absent-mindedly fished around in his vest pocket till he found a match. "They say they'll take him. Shavano is the one who's talking. I figure the rest of them will do what he says. It wouldn't be so bad, you see, if the Utes weren't sore about the deal Ouray and Schurz made last winter in Washington. They figure, and you and I know they're right, that they're going to wind up losing their land here. They signed the agreement, or some of them did, but that doesn't make any difference. The more they think about it, the madder they get. Now that Johnson's been murdered, and on this side of the reservation line to boot, they're ready to start shooting."

"Why did they sign the agreement if they don't like it?"

"Ouray made the deal and he wanted them to accept it. He died thinking they'd all get farms where the Grand and the Gunnison come together which is what the agreement says, but now the Utes think they're going to be moved into Utah. As long as Ouray was alive, they talked low or just got sullen and didn't say anything. Now they're mean and they're not afraid to let everybody know it."

"How long have you got?"

"Not me," Leslie said quickly. "Us! We! Damn it, man, I can't make a decision like this alone. Neither can Ben Harlan. He's down there on the river now talking to Shavano. Lieutenant Avery can't, either. This is something we've got to agree on and then go ahead and do whatever we decide. I can tell you that I'm glad to have a Department of the Interior man here to help make the decision."

"I'd better correct that now," Dave said. "I resigned when I finished my job."

"The hell!" Leslie stared at Dave in the lamplight that fell through the open doorway above them. "Well, that's bad news, but you've been a Department of the Interior man and you've got Carl Schurz's confidence. That helps."

"How much time have we got?"

"Till sunup."

"You've got some soldiers here?"

Leslie laughed, a short, humorless sound. "Lieutenant Avery is here with a detail of six men. Harlan would have done better to have left them at the post. We had a couple of companies here last night, but they were headed for Lake City and they moved out this morning. I'm not sure if that many soldiers would have helped. The Army is supposed to protect the Utes, but it's like it was on White River. The Indians hate the soldiers and they're afraid of them."

"How many Indians are here?"

"Seventy-five anyway. May be more by morning. A lot of braves are out hunting. All of them that were in camp came as soon as they heard what had happened."

"How many white men besides the seven soldiers?"

"I have four men working for me. That's five of us. Seven with you and Harlan. The stage driver and one man passenger makes nine. Sixteen with the soldiers."

"Eighteen with the two freighters."

Leslie started to light his pipe. Now he lowered the match flame and let it die in his hand. He said, "Dave, no matter what happens or what you say, I will not under any circumstances let either one of those bastards have a gun."

Dave shrugged. "All right. I'd like to talk to them after a while. Right now I'm still hungry and I want to see Sharon."

"Sure. I'll talk to Mrs. Patrick. You'll find Miss Morgan in the front upstairs room on the east side."

Dave ran past Leslie into the house and up the stairs. He knocked on Sharon's door, breathing hard and for a moment forgetting that all of them stood in the shadow of death, for now he could think of nothing except that Sharon was here on the other side of this door.

He heard her cross the room. The door opened and she stood before him, the lighted lamp behind her, as tall and regal-looking as ever. Her blond hair hung down her back in a great mass. He had never seen it that way before and he was surprised there was so much of it. She wore a blue robe, the cord tied tightly around her slender waist.

The hall was dark and she did not recognize him until he said, "Sharon, I'm glad I caught up with you."

"Dave," she cried. "Dave honey," and threw herself into his arms.

She hugged him with all her strength; she kissed him with wild abandon, their lips clinging together until they were both out of breath, and then she pulled him into her room and shut the door and stood looking at him.

"I thought I would never see you again, Dave," she said. "I've been about out of my head the last few weeks waiting for you and not knowing when you were coming. I told Major Leslie you'd be here any time and I knew you'd settle this as soon as you got here. It's so crazy, Dave. Major Leslie said he might let those . . . those devils have them. You can save them, can't you?"

"Who?"

"Oh, I thought you knew," she said. "It's Vince and Duke Conway."

Dave sat down on the bed and stared at her. He should have known, he thought dismally. Major Leslie had probably avoided mentioning their names purposely. He knew what Dave thought of Conway. But Vince! He shook his head, thinking that this was what Vince got for hooking up with a man like Duke Conway.

Now, seeing the expression on Sharon's face, he knew he had to walk a tightrope if he expected to marry her.

11

Dave rose and walked to the window and stared into the darkness, his back to Sharon. She came to him and slipped her arms around him. She said, "You won't let him turn them over to the Indians, will you?"

"I don't have any authority," he said. "I never expected to run into this kind of a mess, so I resigned before I left Santa Fe."

"I don't see that it makes any difference," she said. "Major Leslie respects your judgment. He told me he did. It's that . . . that terrible man Harlan I'm worried about. All he thinks about are his Indians." Suddenly she smiled. "I'm glad you quit your job. This is better. If you aren't working for Schurz, you won't have to take the Indians' side any more."

Dave was silent, thinking how little she understood his convictions, and then he thought of Johnson, a friendly boy who had not been more than seventeen, and of Duke Conway who had boasted drunkenly in Cleora that time about making a good Indian out of a live one if he ever had a chance. Well, he'd had a chance and he'd done exactly what he'd wanted to regardless of justice or what the consequences of his act would be.

"Dave," she said sharply, stepping back from him, "I don't understand you. You surely aren't worried about me or Mrs. Patrick. We're the only women here and there are no children. We'll be all right if there is trouble. There are enough men around to protect us. It's Vince and Conway I'm thinking about. You would never consent to giving them up to the Indians, would you?"

He turned then and looked at her, the pleasure of seeing

her again suddenly gone from him. It was as if he had held something in his hands that was very rare and beautiful, and now had turned to ashes. Her judgment had been made; to her the situation was a matter of black and white and she would never understand how it could be anything else to him.

"I don't know right now what I'd consent to," he said slowly. "I haven't talked to Conway or Vince, or to Ben Harlan. When I came in, he was with the Indians."

She was angry. He saw it in her eyes, in the red spots that appeared in her cheeks, in the slight tremble of the corners of her mouth. Her hands were clenched into tight fists at her sides. She said, "Dave, you're a white man. Conway and Vince are white men. You couldn't possibly think of turning them over to savages to be tortured to death because one filthy Indian boy was killed in self-defense."

"If it was really self-defense, I would not consent to giving him up," Dave said. "I guess I wouldn't anyhow because even Conway has the right of a trial by jury, but I'm not sure what the proper procedure for us is. First we've got to find out the truth about what happened when Johnson was killed if we can."

"Truth," she cried. "Dave, we know the truth."

"How?"

"Vince told me," she said. "So did Conway. There's no question about it. This Indian boy rode into camp and threatened them because they wouldn't feed him. Then when he started to ride off he turned around and was going to shoot. If Conway hadn't fired, he'd have been killed. Vince, too, or maybe both of them."

"That isn't the way Young Bucks tells it," Dave said.

"The other Indian boy? You'd consider believing a savage instead of them?"

"I might," Dave said, "knowing what the stakes are and knowing a little bit about Conway."

"All right, Conway's no good," she said. "He'd lie to save his neck, but Vince wouldn't. You know that."

He didn't know it, but he didn't tell Sharon that. He looked at her, sensing the pent-up fury that was about to explode, and he remembered what she had told him about her temper and her perverse disposition. She would regret tomorrow what she was about to say tonight, but by then it would have been said and it could not be taken back.

In this short, vibrant moment he thought of the disagreements they'd had over the Utes and how closed her mind was on the subject, an attitude that never seemed to fit with the rest of her character as he saw it. He had told himself in the past that this difficulty was not an important one, that once they were away from Ute country the subject would never come up.

Now he knew he had been wrong, that it was a basic difference in their attitude toward life and their fellow men and it would come up again and again in different ways. But the part that hurt was Sharon's obvious determination to turn this moment of reunion which he had been looking forward to for so long into a quarrel that could have been avoided.

He saw that she was tapping her right foot on the floor, that her anger was steadily mounting until she had almost reached the explosion point. He said quickly, "Sharon, I think you can quit worrying about Vince. From what Leslie told me, I doubt that his life is in any more danger than ours. It's Conway they want."

"Even Conway's a civilized white man," she said harshly. "His life is worth a dozen savages."

There it was, he thought bitterly, the whole trouble between them stated briefly. Sharon had said what most Colorado people would say. In effect she was contending that a white man could do no wrong and an Indian could do no right. He was reminded of Ouray's remark that by white men's standards it was all right for a white to rape a Ute woman, but it was unforgivable for a Ute to rape a white woman.

He turned toward the door. "Mrs. Patrick is fixing some supper for me. Want to come down and have a cup of coffee?"

The red spots were still in her cheeks, the corners of her mouth were still trembling, her foot was still tapping its angry message on the floor. She said coldly, "No, you go ahead. When you make up your mind what you're going to do, let me know.''

''All right,'' he said, and left the room.

As soon as he sat down at the dining-room table, Mrs. Patrick brought a plate from the kitchen piled high with a sizzling steak, fried potatoes, and beans. She set it in front of him as she said, ''I'm glad to see you, Mr. Rand. Miss Morgan was hoping you would come.''

''I'm glad to get here and have a chance at your good cooking,'' he said, ''but I apologize for putting you to so much trouble.''

''I wouldn't do it for anyone else,'' she said, winking at him. ''Besides, I didn't have anything else to do and it looks like we're going to be up all night.''

She went back into the kitchen and returned with a plate of hot biscuits and a pot of coffee. As she poured the coffee, she asked, ''How does it look to you?''

He didn't want to alarm her, but he didn't want to lie to her, either. He said, ''I guess you know the Indians better than I do.''

''If you ask me, I'd say we're in a tight squeeze,'' she said. ''I've been feeding some of the beggars all summer, seems like. They used to be good natured and they'd laugh and joke when they were here, but for the last month since Ouray died they've been mean. I've been afraid of them every time they stopped.''

He nodded thoughtfully. ''You know, Mrs. Patrick, if I was in their place, I'd be mean, too.''

''Oh, so would I,'' she agreed, ''but that don't make me feel one bit better. Just because my hair is turning white is no reason for me to lose it.''

He grinned. ''No, I guess it isn't.''

She brought him a slab of custard pie. He was finishing it when Leslie came in. Dave asked, ''Harlan come back yet?''

''No, and I don't like it. The Indians will dicker with him if they'll dicker with anybody. They trust him. He puts them ahead of everything else and I think he's honest about it.'' A hint of humor crept into his eyes. ''He knows that Carl Schurz sent him here to do exactly that and he knows he won't last long if he doesn't.'' The humor faded and he asked, ''You've talked to Miss Morgan?''

Dave nodded, sitting back in his chair and reaching into his coat pocket for a cigar. ''It's very simple the way she sees it. We don't give Conway to the Indians. If they attack us, we are strong enough to protect her and Mrs. Patrick.''

''I knew she felt that,'' Leslie said. ''She's right about Conway, I guess, but protecting the women against an attack is something else. Indians would burn the house and kill us as we ran out of it.'' He paused, his gaze swinging around the room. ''It'd be hell to lose all this, Dave. I've got the start of a good ranch here. I'd hate to begin from scratch again if I lived through it.''

''Any chance of slipping the women out?''

''Not any. Shavano's got the buildings surrounded so tight you couldn't blow your breath through his lines.''

''I didn't see any of them when I came in.''

''They were there.''

''Where's Conway and Kelso?''

''I've got them under guard in the bar.''

''I'd like to talk to them.''

Leslie rose and jerked his head for Dave to follow. ''They won't change their story, but it won't hurt for you to talk to them.''

As he followed Leslie out of the dining room, he asked himself how Sharon could be two people, the one he loved who was sweet and kind and good, the other who took over the moment the Utes were mentioned, a hard and bitter woman he could not even like. He had no answer that made any sense.

The stage driver and another man Dave guessed was the passenger who had come in with Sharon were sitting at a table on one side of the bar. When Leslie stepped into the room he motioned toward the door and the two men rose and walked out. Kelso and Conway were sitting at another table. One of Leslie's men was leaning against the pine bar, his revolver beside him on the wide plank. He picked up the revolver when Leslie nodded at him, holstered it, and left.

When Kelso recognized Dave, he let out a whoop and jumped up and ran across the room, his hand extended. "By God, I never seen a more welcome sight in my life than you are, Dave. Sharon said you'd be along any time, but I figured you'd be too late."

Dave shook hands. "I'm glad to see you, Vince. She didn't know when I'd show up. I just got in a little while ago." He looked at the man's eager face. It was pale and drawn, a nervous tic had developed in his right cheek, and his eyes had fear in them, something Dave had never sensed in him before.

For a moment Kelso's gaze was on Dave's face as if seeking assurance, then he glanced back at Conway. He said, "Dave, I want you to meet Duke Conway. I know you've heard a lot about him."

Conway rose and held out his hand. "Pleased to meet-cha, Rand. I've sure heard a lot about you."

"Sit down," Dave said. "I've heard about you, too, Conway. I wouldn't shake hands with you if my life depended on it."

A sudden, wild rage turned Conway's big face purple. "Why, God damn you for an Injun-loving bastard. I'll beat you to death."

He started toward Dave but stopped after he'd taken two steps. Leslie, standing slightly behind Dave and to one side of him, had drawn his gun. He said, "Conway, I don't like you any better than Rand does. If you lay a hand on him, I'll kill you. Believe me, I hope you do because if you were dead we'd be out of a pile of trouble."

Conway sat down, glaring at Leslie. He said thickly, "You're as bad as Rand. You're both Injun-lovers. A man couldn't expect justice out of either one of you."

"Justice?" Dave asked softly. "Did you give Johnson any justice?"

"Johnson? The Indian kid?" Conway seemed puzzled. "What are you making a big stink about him for? He was just a Ute."

"To you he's an animal," Dave said. "That right?"

Conway shrugged his beefy shoulders. "Maybe not an animal, but when you think of Father Meeker and those men up there at White River that they killed, it seems to me they acted like animals."

"Johnson wasn't there," Dave said.

He turned away, red spots dancing before his eyes. He had to fight an almost uncontrollable impulse to reach out and throttle the man. Duke Conway or hardly anyone else in Colorado knew what actually had happened at White River. Some even had been critical of Nathan Meeker before the massacre, but the instant he was murdered he became "Father Meeker." Perhaps he deserved the title, but for a man like Duke Conway to use it in a thinly disguised effort to clear himself of murder was too much.

"I don't see what that's got to do with it," Conway said in an aggrieved tone. "The Utes done it and Johnson was a Ute."

Kelso returned to his table and sat down. He said, "Dave, I'm sorry it happened, but what kind of a fool would Duke have been if he'd stood there and let the Ute kid shoot him? I'd have been next."

Dave swung around to face Conway. The freighter had the network of red lines in his face of a hard drinker. He had not shaved for several days, he had a horse stink about him, not the smell of a rider but that of a livery stable hostler who never washes. He had a big yellow pimple at the base of his nose. His eyes were bloodshot and now he stared at Dave in the belligerent manner of a man who was being put upon.

Suddenly it struck Dave that Conway was stupid as well as immoral. That was the difference between him and Kelso. Conway even now did not have the slightest feeling that he had done anything wrong, but Kelso knew a wrong had been done and that, Dave thought, was the reason he was scared.

"Conway," Dave said, "tell me exactly what happened."

"I can sure do that," the freighter said, "and I can do it quick. It was real early. Sun wasn't up yet. I'd taken care of the horses and Vince was getting breakfast when them bastards rode into camp. The one they call Johnson wanted something to eat and I said to get out. I told 'em we didn't feed beggars. They could go to the agency and get a handout. The government's got plenty of money to feed them murdering sons of bitches, but me, I can work my tail off and pay taxes for the privilege.

"Well, they didn't move very fast, so I got my rifle. I told 'em they'd better git, and then this Johnson got mean. He shook his rifle in my face and he levered a shell into the chamber like he meant business. But he didn't have the guts to fight me face to face. He got on his horse and rode off a piece, then he turned around and was fixing to shoot me, but I expected that and I got him first. They both rode off into the quakies and we didn't see no more of 'em.''

"Why did you and Vince come here to Major Leslie's place?'' Dave asked.

Conway looked at the top of the table as he fumbled in his coat pocket for a cigar. "We didn't figure I'd done any more than wing the kid, but Vince and me got to talking. We knowed how ornery the Injuns have been all summer and Vince said we'd have the whole bunch of Uncompahgres down on us afore we'd gone ten miles, so we decided we'd better come here.''

"You knew you'd be safe with Major Leslie?''

"Yeah, we figured so.'' Conway glared at Leslie, his lower lip jutting forward like a sullen child. "I didn't think he'd hold us like we was criminals or something.''

"The Indian story doesn't match yours,'' Dave said.

"You think they'd tell the truth?'' Conway shook his head and stared at Dave as if he thought he was crazy. "Are you telling me you'd believe an Injun kid instead of a white man?''

Dave threw up his hands in disgust. "If you're saying that white men always tell the truth and Indians always lie, you're a bigger fool than I thought you were.'' He turned to Leslie. "Is this exactly the same story he's told before?''

"The same,'' Leslie said.

"All right, Vince, now tell me what happened,'' Dave ordered.

"Oh, come off it,'' Kelso said peevishly. "You've just heard what happened. No sense me going over it.''

"You're saying it happened exactly the way Conway told it?"

"Sure."

Kelso looked Dave squarely in the eyes when he said it. Dave still didn't believe it, and it was his opinion that Kelso was afraid of Conway. Or perhaps he wanted to keep his job if they lived through it. Or—and this thought shocked Dave—there was a possibility that Kelso knew he would be well thought of by Sharon if he helped keep Conway from being turned over to the Indians.

Dave scratched his head, glancing at Leslie who was watching him. "Did it ever occur to you, Conway, that by coming here you were putting Major Leslie and his men and Mrs. Patrick in great danger?" Dave asked.

Conway snorted. "Naw, the Injuns like him. They won't hurt him or anybody who works for him."

Leslie laughed shortly. "Well, Conway, there's one way I can keep them liking me. That's to turn you over to them. They say we've got till sunup."

"You won't do no such thing," Conway said. "No white man would ever turn another white man over to a god-damned Injun, and you're a white man even if you are an Injun lover."

Leslie took a long breath. "We're in a squeeze and that's a fact," he admitted.

"You've got no call to make prisoners out of us, neither," Kelso said angrily. "We've got a right to have a drink or anything else we want."

"I think Vince is right, Major," Dave said. "Turn them loose. You don't have any authority to hold them as prisoners."

Surprised, Leslie opened his mouth to say something, then he saw what Dave was getting at, and he nodded. Without a word he started toward the door.

"Hey, wait," Conway yelled.

Leslie stopped and looked back. "I was going to get your horses. We'll let you leave."

"Oh no, you ain't turning us loose for them devils to torture," Conway shouted. "We wouldn't ride a mile till they had us."

"I thought you were kicking about being prisoners?"

"No, we ain't kicking one bit," Conway said. "This is fine. We like it here, don't we, Vince?"

"Yeah," Kelso muttered. "We like it just fine." He looked at Dave. "You got something against me because of Sharon? You told me to look out for her and I done it. I didn't lay a hand on her, neither. She's been waiting for you."

"No, I don't have anything against you, Vince," Dave answered. "Nothing except working for Conway. When you decide to change your story about what happened this morning, send for me."

"What are you going to do with us?" Conway demanded.

"I don't know," Leslie said.

"Neither do I," Dave said, "but I don't favor fighting the Indians off in the morning to save your worthless neck. If we don't turn you over to them, it looks like that's what we'll have to do. You might just as well know we haven't got much chance it if comes to a fight. Why don't you give yourself up to them, Conway? That would save the rest of us including the two women who are in the house."

For the first time Conway seemed to grasp the fact that he really was in danger. He half-rose from his chair, then dropped back. His big hands, palm down on the table, began to shake.

"No," Conway said. "I won't do it."

"That's what I thought," Dave said. "Come on, Major. No use listening to anything they've got to say unless they want to tell a different story."

Dave walked out of the bar into the hall. Leslie called his man back to stand guard over Conway and Kelso. Dave said, "Why keep a guard with them? They won't go anywhere."

"I don't want them floating around through the house where they can get their hands on some guns," Leslie said, "or get into any devilment. I don't want them getting drunk, either. After a while I'll move them, maybe let them go to bed upstairs. What do you want to do now?"

"I want to talk to Young Bucks."

Leslie nodded. "I thought you would. All right, we'll go get our horses."

Before Dave and Leslie reached the stable, Mike Collins stepped out of the shadows. He said, "Harlan just got back."

"You haven't seen or heard anything?" Leslie asked.

"Not a thing," Collins answered, "but they're out there watching us. The way my skin's crawling I know they are."

"We won't have any trouble till sunup," Leslie said. "I never knew Shavano to break his word."

Harlan stepped out of the stall and stood under the lantern hanging over the door, his gaze on Leslie. He asked suspiciously, "Where you going?"

"We thought we'd have a talk with Young Bucks," Leslie said.

Dave moved forward so that the lantern light fell on his face. He said, "How are you, Harlan?"

The agent stared at him a moment before he recognized him, then he said, "I didn't know you'd got here, Rand," and held out his hand.

"I rode in a little while ago," Dave said as he shook hands. "I was the one who wanted to talk to Young Bucks."

"Don't do it," Harlan warned. "Leave 'em alone till morning. I've been with Shavano since before dark. I've never seen him like this before. Or the rest of 'em, either. They're sullen. Don't want to talk. I've known these men for several years, the older ones anyhow. I wouldn't have taken the agent job if I hadn't thought I knew what I was getting into. Well, gentlemen, I didn't know."

"What are you trying to say, Ben?" Leslie asked.

Harlan took a long breath. "I'm saying that there ain't much standing between us and another White River massacre. You know what Colorow and Jack and some of the others said after the Milk Creek scrap? They allowed that if they were going to be sent to Indian Territory, they'd rather be killed fighting than to go on living. Shavano and Sapinero and most of the Uncompahgres feel the same way about going to Utah, but I figure they wouldn't have got up enough nerve to make trouble if that bastardly Conway hadn't murdered Shavano's son. That's just what we need to set this off unless they get Conway.''

"We can't turn him over to them, Ben," Leslie said. "You know that as well as I do even if we had proof it really was murder."

"It was murder, all right," Harlan said angrily. "I know Young Bucks. I've had him tell his story half a dozen times and it's always the same. They rode into Conway's camp and asked for biscuits. Conway called them sons of bitches and said to get out before he killed 'em. Johnson said they weren't sons of bitches. He was sore, all right, but Young Bucks says he was polite. He told Conway it was a long ways to camp and asked again for a biscuit.

"Kelso was standing by the fire. He said to Conway they had a few biscuits left from the night before and it would be a good idea to give 'em to the boys, but Conway cussed him and cussed the boys, then he cocked his rifle and said for 'em to ride. When they started off, Johnson told Young Bucks they'd probably get shot in the back. He looked around once. That was when Conway fired. Johnson stayed on the horse long enough to get out of sight in the quakies and that was all. He died a little while after that."

Dave, listening, did not doubt that this was the truth. Still, in any Colorado court the young Indian's story would not stand up against Kelso's and Conway's testimony. Shavano was familiar enough with white men's ways to know that, so even if he was told that Conway would be taken to Gunnison and tried, he would be unlikely to let it go at that.

"Well, what do we do?" Dave asked.

Harlan wiped his face with his handkerchief and stuffed it into his pocket. "I don't agree with Major Leslie. I say we can turn Conway over to them."

"No," Dave said. "He's got a right to a trial the same as any citizen of the United States. He wouldn't live long enough to be tried if the Utes had him because to them he's already been found guilty of murder."

"Hell, he is guilty," Harlan snapped. "Now look here, both of you. If we don't give him up, what else can we do? If we move him to the fort or the agency, he'll be under the Indians' noses. They'll take him and they'll kill him and they'll kill anybody who tries to stop 'em. If we sit tight here and tell 'em we won't give Conway up, they'll attack the house at sunup and they'll burn it. We can't stay in a burning house. They'll shoot us down like rabbits while we're running for cover."

Harlan wagged a forefinger under Dave's nose. "You ought to know a little about Indians by now. Once they've killed a bunch of whites, they'll go hog wild. They'll raid the towns along the edge of the reservation and they'll kill hundreds of people before enough soldiers could get here to stop 'em. That would have happened last fall after the Meeker massacre if it hadn't been for Ouray. Right there's the difference. Ouray won't be holding 'em back no more."

"The last part of what you said is right," Leslie agreed. "I'm not so sure about the rest."

"You're sure enough," Harlan said sharply. "I've talked to Mrs. Patrick. She told me how the Utes have acted when they stopped here to eat. She says she's been scared every time. How about you, Sam? You haven't been?"

Leslie grinned. "I don't like to admit it, but I guess I have been a little."

Mike Collins had been listening. He said, "I'll admit it, Major. I've been more'n a little scared, and I never thought I would be scared of the Uncompahgres. I worked at the Los Pinos Agency one year helping with the agency herd and I got to liking several of 'em. They'd help with the cattle and they didn't make no trouble."

"That's right," Harlan said, "but now they're like ornery kids walking around with chips on their shoulders. If we let this go, they'll knock the chips off themselves and come a-shooting by sunup."

"Then we'll have to shoot back," Dave said.

"There's more to think about," Harlan said stubbornly. "If we let an outbreak start here, we'll have one all over

the country. The Southern Utes will rise. So will the
Apaches. You know what Victorio's been doing. The
Navajos will join 'em. Don't think they're happy down
there on that desert they live on. And don't forget the
Mormons. They'll help the Indians if it's only seeing they
have guns and ammunition. I tell you we'll start the damned-
est Indian war this country ever seen and all because of a
no-good drunk freighter you fellows want to protect.''

Dave hadn't thought it was that serious. He glanced at
Leslie and saw that he was considering what Harlan had
said, too. Dave said slowly, ''If we give Conway to them,
they'll go home and that will be the end of it?''

Harlan nodded. ''Shavano promised that's what they'd
do. All he wants is to be sure that Johnson's murderer is
punished.''

''I can tell you one thing,'' Collins said sourly. ''If
Conway wasn't Conway, I'd say to hold out and fight, but
I don't cotton to the notion of losing my life saving his.''

''I don't like him any better than you do,'' Dave said,
''but I tell you we can't hand him over to the Utes.''

''Not even to save Miss Morgan's life?'' Collins
demanded.

''No, not even for that.''

''My God!'' Harlan threw up his hands. ''You put one
man's life, a man we know is a murderer, above all the
lives including women and children that will be lost in an
Indian war? You're a fool, Rand.''

''We'd better consider something else,'' Leslie said.
''Maybe it isn't an honorable motive, but we'd better think
about it just the same. If we turn Conway over to the Utes
and they murder him as we know they will, do you have
any idea what the people of this state will do to us?''

''Nothing,'' Harlan snapped. ''We're living on an Indian reservation. They couldn't touch us. If any legal
action is taken, it would be in a Federal court.''

''They'll touch us, all right,'' Leslie said, ''whether
they have the authority or not.''

Dave was only half-listening. He was thinking of Sharon
and how she felt and what she would say. Then he remembered something his mother had said to him when he was a

small boy. He had not thought of it for years, but it was in his mind now as clearly as if he had heard the words only yesterday: "You were born into a cruel world, David, and there are times when you have to be hard to journey through it, but be sure of one thing. Be proud of your journey. Don't live in a way that will make you ashamed of it later."

Now, looking at Harlan, Dave wondered how much the fear for his own life was forcing the agent to take the stand he did. Dave could not be proud of himself if he let Ben Harlan have his way. Or if he did what Sharon asked simply because he wanted her to go on loving him. Or if he thought about what the people of the state would do if Conway was given to the Indians.

"It's all right for us to think about alternatives," Dave said, "but in the end there's only one principle that counts. If we let anything else guide us in making a decision, we are as bad as Conway."

"What is the principle?" Harlan asked suspiciously.

"Last fall when Carl Schurz appointed the commission to hold hearings at the Los Pinos Agency," Dave said, "he put Ouray on the commission. His instructions were to treat the Utes as if they were white men, at least to see that they have the same rights. Now Conway has murdered an Indian, and he's got to be tried for murder the same as an Indian would be tried if he had murdered a white man."

Harlan cursed with deep feeling, then he shoved his face close to Dave's. "You idiot, you know that no jury will ever find a white man guilty of murdering an Indian."

"He still has the right to be tried," Dave said. "Major, I have an idea I think is worth trying. Mike, saddle my horse. Saddle one of Major Leslie's if he's willing to take a chance on losing him."

"Sure," Leslie said. "Saddle Blacky. It won't break me if I lose him."

"If I come back with Kelso," Dave said to Collins, "I want you to talk scary. And Harlan, you stay out of sight."

Turning, Dave strode toward the house. Leslie hesitated, then caught up with him. He said, "Harlan didn't tell you, but he was scared after Young Bucks brought Johnson's body in. Shavano and most of the Utes rode to the agency whooping and yelling and shaking their rifles in his face like maniacs. That's why he brought the soldiers. He's been scared ever since." Leslie paused, and added, "I'm not sure we can blame him. I've seen the Utes worked up like that a few times and I can say from my own experience that it's a terrifying experience."

"I blame any man who lets fear dictate his decision on anything as important as this," Dave said, "and I think that's what he's doing."

"Maybe," Leslie said. "What are you up to with Kelso?"

"I'm going to get the truth out of him," Dave said. "I want you to move Conway out of the bar. Your office would be a good place to keep him."

Leslie hesitated, stopping in front of the house and teetering back and forth on his toes as he stared at the sky. Finally he said, "Sunup is coming before we want it to get here. I'll move Conway, and I sure hope you know what you're doing."

12

When Dave and Leslie reached the bar, Leslie said to his man who was guarding Conway and Kelso, "Jake, take Conway to my office. I want to talk to him alone."

"I ain't going," Conway said angrily. "You ain't gonna separate us. We've been together all along . . ."

"And you're both involved," Dave said. "It's like the old saying about you'll hang together or you'll hang separately. That it?"

"We ain't neither one of us gonna hang," Conway muttered. "You take me to Gunnison and throw me into jail and have me tried and I'll go free. You know it as well as I do."

"I wish I had you there right now and these Indians off our backs," Leslie said, "but you're not there and the Indians have the place surrounded. Harlan just got back from talking to Shavano and the old man won't back up an inch." He motioned to the door. "I told you what you were doing. Get out of that chair and move."

Jake walked around Conway and stood behind him, his cocked revolver lined on the back of Conway's head. He said, "This iron has got an awful easy trigger, Conway. Sometimes just a quick move will make it go off."

Conway looked at Jake and then at Leslie and he began to curse in a whining tone. He cried out in a voice that was strangely high-pitched for so big a man, "You'd give me to those red devils just to save your own necks, wouldn't you?"

"Is your neck worth saving at the expense of ours?" Dave asked.

Conway didn't answer. He got to his feet, glancing at

Kelso and hesitated, acting as if he wanted to say something, but decided not to. He walked out of the bar, Jake and Leslie following him.

"I guess the Major wouldn't begrudge us one drink, Vince," Dave said.

"Not if he don't know about it," Kelso said. "I'm sure dry."

Dave brought a bottle and two glasses from the bar, filled the glasses, and took the bottle back. He returned to the table and, sitting down, lifted his glass. "Here's to a long life for all of us."

"I can drink to that." Kelso lifted his glass and drank, then set the glass back on the table. "What was Leslie's idea taking Conway back to his office?"

"I asked him to. I wanted to talk to you alone." Dave offered Kelso a cigar and lighted one for himself. He pulled on it a moment, his gaze on Kelso, then he went on, "We've talked about this before, but it's more surprising now. I mean, you and me and Sharon all being on the train and then riding the stage to this place. Both of us falling in love with Sharon and then getting thrown together here again. It's too strange to be coincidence. I've never been sure what makes a man's destiny, but something is at work we don't understand."

Kelso was suspicious and had been from the time Conway had left. He chewed on his cigar, then gripped it firmly in the right side of his mouth and spoke around it. He said, "Whenever you give me a mess of your highfalutin talk, I know damned well that trouble's coming. Now what is it?"

"Maybe no trouble," Dave said. "I'm just thinking about us two and Sharon. I guess if it came to a proposition of saving her life, either one of us or both would be willing to give ours up if we knew it would do the job."

Still suspicious, Kelso frowned as he considered what Dave had said. Finally he nodded. "Sure we would."

"I thought so," Dave said blandly. "Now the answer to our problem is simple. The Utes want the man who killed Johnson. If they get him, they'll go back to their camp and they won't give us any more trouble. Harlan just told us that Shavano had promised him that's what they'd do. According to Young Bucks, Conway murdered Johnson, but before we give Conway up, I've got to be sure. I want the truth out of you.''

"You had it,'' Kelso said. "He told you what had happened and I said it was true.''

"And I say you're a liar, Vince,'' Dave shot back. "I think you're afraid of him. Or you want to keep your job if Conway gets out of this alive. Or maybe you're lying because you know it's what Sharon wants you to say.''

"You're accusing Sharon of wanting me to lie to save Conway's hide?'' Kelso asked. "Oh no, you got her wrong.''

"I didn't say she wanted you to lie, but she wants Conway's story to be the truth so bad that she can't let herself think for a minute that it might be any other way.''

Kelso thought about it for a time, then nodded grudgingly. "I reckon that's right. She hates the Utes more'n Duke does. She talked to me a lot when you was gone. She got so damned lonesome. She missed you and I didn't seem to fill the bill. She likes everything about you except your attitude toward the Utes. Finally she got it into her head that after while you'd hate the Utes, too, and it wouldn't be a cause of trouble between you.''

"I'd never hate the Utes,'' Dave said. "Sharon knows that.''

He stared at Kelso, thinking he must be lying, then he realized that the man was telling the truth, that it was exactly how Sharon would rationalize. She couldn't change and she couldn't give Dave up, so he was the one who would have to change. But all this time he had been telling himself that she would change when they were out of the Ute country. That was the irony of it, he thought. His thinking had been the opposite of hers because he knew he would not change and he could not give her up, so in his mind she was the one who would have to change.

He rose and walked the length of the room, pulling steadily on his cigar. Hate was a kind of sickness, he thought, and he guessed it was why he had the feeling that Sharon was two girls, the one he loved and the one he didn't like. Now, standing at a window and staring into the blackness, he knew that he would marry the Sharon he loved if she would have him, but in the years to come the other Sharon would be there the instant she was reminded of the Utes.

"I don't mind admitting I tried to take advantage of you being away," Kelso said, "but I never got anywhere. I kept telling her that you two could never get along and she'n me could. She'd just say she loved you and that ended it."

Dave turned and strode back to the table. He said harshly, "We got off the subject. Now you write out a statement about what happened and sign it. I want the truth, not Conway's lies."

Kelso shook his head. "Not me. I'd be responsible for Conway's death and Sharon would hate me just like she's gonna hate you. Besides, I won't have no part of turning him over to the Utes."

"Not even to save Sharon's life?"

"No," Kelso said. "I don't think it will come down to that."

"It hasn't yet, but it will at sunup," Dave said, "and that's not very far away."

"I don't believe it," Kelso said. "They talk a lot, but when it comes to attacking a solid house like this, with fifteen or twenty of us inside shooting 'em to pieces, they'll back off in a hurry."

"All right, there's another way," Dave said. "Come on."

"What are you fixing to do?"

"I'll tell you," Dave said impatiently. "Come on."

"I ain't budging," Kelso said.

Dave had started toward the door. Now he turned back to stand across the table from Kelso. He said, "Vince, we've been through quite a bit together. At times we've hated each other, I guess, and there have been a few times we came pretty close to fighting. I remember you invited me outside the night we were in Cleora. Still, I think we've respected each other and because we did, we've been friends."

Kelso nodded gravely. "That's right. You don't know how much I hated you New Year's Eve when you two told me you were engaged, but even then I figured that if it wasn't going to be me, it had better be you."

"Vince, I don't want our friendship to come to an end," Dave leaned forward. "I don't like to make threats, but I propose to keep them from attacking this house. If I can, Sharon will be safe. Now you're coming with me, one way or another."

For a moment Kelso sat as if frozen, his eyes locked with Dave's, then he rose. Without a word Dave strode to the door and out of the house, Kelso following. When they reached the stable, Collins stepped into the lantern light and motioned toward the hitch rail.

"I saddled the horses like you told me," Collins said, "but I dunno why you want to ride tonight. You won't get half a mile." A coyote barked from a ridge top between the Cimarron and the Black Canyon. Collins jerked a hand to the north. "Hear that? They're all around here."

"How big an idiot do you think I am?" Kelso said testily. "That was a genuwine coyote."

"Think so?" Collins chuckled. "You think what you damn please, but I know a Ute when I hear one, and I've been hearing 'em all night. You and Dave go ahead and ride. It's your hair you're risking, not mine."

"Where we going?" Kelso demanded of Dave.

"There's two ways we can maybe save Sharon's life," Dave said, "and my idea is to use both of them so that if one doesn't work maybe the other one will. If we stand pat, we're all dead, but there's a slim chance we might get through to the Army post in time and get back with enough men to whip the Indians."

"And if we don't?" Kelso asked.

"Then they've got us," Dave said. "Maybe we'd be enough to satisfy them."

"You ain't done nothing," Kelso said. "I ain't, neither. I don't savvy this fool play. Conway's the one they want. He killed the boy."

"But they might settle for us," Dave said. "For you anyway. You were standing there when Johnson was shot.

You could have stopped it. They know that, so when they figure they're going to pay a big price to get Conway, they'll take you because you're cheap and better than nothing.''

Kelso stood motionless, a pulse hammering in his forehead, his lips quivering. Collins said, ''It's gonna be hell for you, Kelso. I'm glad it ain't me. You know what they'll do? They'll make you pay for every crime that's been committed against them for the last ten years. They'll spread-eagle you and they'll cut you. They'll trim off your ears and your nose and your eyelids and . . .''

''Shut up,'' Kelso screamed. ''My God, shut up.'' He whirled to face Dave. ''All right, all right, I'll tell you how it was. The boys rode into camp peaceful enough and asked for some biscuits. I told Duke we'd better give 'em some, but he'd been drinking and he cussed 'em and he cussed me and said if they didn't get out he'd shoot both of 'em, so they rode off. Just as Johnson turned to look back, Duke let him have it.''

Dave handed a notebook and pencil to Kelso. ''Write it out and sign it. You don't need to put down all you just told us. What we have to have is your statement that you were an eyewitness and that it was murder. If I had it, there wouldn't be any need for us to ride out tonight.''

Kelso squatted under the lantern and wrote slowly and painfully in a quavery hand: *I seen Duke Conway shoot Johnson. It was murder. The boy was leaving camp. Conway had no reason to kill him. Vince Kelso.*

He rose and handed the notebook to Dave. He was crying and shaking, and saliva was running down his chin. He tried to say something, but all he could do was to make an incoherent, animal-like sound.

''All right, Vince,'' Dave said. ''We'll go back into the house. Mike, unsaddle the horses.''

Kelso walked beside Dave to the house, stumbling and almost falling several times. He was still sobbing and half choking. Dave, looking at him, was ashamed. He had set out to break him and he had. He had not known any other way to do it.

When they reached the door into the bar, Dave said, "Go back in there. I'll ask the major to give you a room."

Dave went along the hall to Leslie's office and opened the door. Leslie and Jake were with Conway. Dave said, "Conway, I have Kelso's signed statement telling what happened. Along with Young Bucks' testimony it will be enough to hang you."

"Go to hell," Conway jeered. "You'll never get a rope on my neck and you know it."

"We'll see," Dave said. "Major, I'd like to talk to you."

Leslie rose and, stepping into the hall, closed the door. Dave said, "Let's keep Conway in here." He showed the notebook to Leslie who read Kelso's statement and nodded.

"Will it work?" Leslie asked.

"I don't know," Dave admitted, "but it might convince Shavano. I couldn't think of anything else to do." He paused, and added, "And it just might hang Conway. Depends on who gets on the jury. Folks don't like anybody going out of their way to stir up Indian trouble. I mean the ones who live close enough to the reservation to lose their hair."

Leslie glanced at his watch. "It's after one. It'll be a long three, four hours till dawn. I guess we'll know then."

"I left Kelso in the bar," Dave said. "I thought you'd better give him a room. Chances are by now he's nursing a whisky bottle."

"I'll take care of him," Leslie said.

Dave waited in the hall until Kelso left the bar with Leslie. Kelso did not look at him as he stumbled past. Dave, watching as he climbed the stairs, knew that they should never call each other friend again.

Dave was standing in front of the house when Leslie came back down the stairs. He saw Dave and stepped outside, asking, "What are you doing?"

"Looking at the dark and not seeing anything," Dave said. "Listening and not hearing anything."

"They're like that," Leslie said. "Sometimes you'll be just riding along and all the time you know you're being watched but you don't see them and you don't hear them."

"It's like that now," Dave said. "I feel the way Mike Collins did a while ago. I know they're out there by the way my skin's crawling."

He was silent a moment, thinking back over this past year from the time Carl Schurz had given him a job as Special Agent. He went on, "Major, I don't scare unless I'm getting a pretty good smell of death. You've been through a lot more of this than I have, so maybe you've got used to it, but when something gets tight enough to scare me, I get a crazy feeling, a kind of a chill racing up and down my spine. I felt it when we were in Douglas's lodge dickering for the prisoners, I had it in the stable at the agency when Colorow threw his knife into the floor and I'm feeling it now."

"No, I never get used to it," Leslie said thoughtfully. "When a man tells you he doesn't scare, he's either a fool or a liar. I feel it, too. I'm a widower. I don't have any children. If I'm killed this morning, I guess there's nobody on God's earth who would sit down and cry for me. I feel sometimes that I've wasted my life, but I don't want to die. Maybe that's the reason. I guess I want another chance to amount to something."

Dave didn't think he'd wasted his life, but he didn't want to die any more than Sam Leslie did. He should have many years ahead of him, years to be married and raise a family, years to publish a newspaper and be a part of a community and stand for something before all men. That was one side of the coin, the side of hope and ambition and happiness; the other side was the grim knowledge that any gambler would give long odds he would be dead within a matter of hours.

"We wouldn't run even for that chance you're talking about," Dave said thoughtfully, "but what will Harlan do? And Lieutenant Avery?"

"They'll go back to the agency with the soldiers as soon as it's daylight," Leslie said. "I think it's the right thing to do. The lieutenant hasn't got enough men to do any good, and if we can convince Shavano that it's to his interest to take Conway to Gunnison for trial, the fact that the soldiers are gone will be in our favor. We've got to go on the basis that we trust him, then he might trust us."

"Maybe we ought to go see him."

Leslie shook his head. "No, he'll be here before sunup. It's best that he comes to us. We'll tell him what we're going to do. After that only God knows what will happen, but we can't take a chance on forting up in the house. There's no sense in throwing Miss Morgan's and Mrs. Patrick's lives away along with ours, and that's what would happen."

Mrs. Patrick called from the doorway. "I've got hot coffee and I've baked a cake. Anybody want some?"

"We sure do," Leslie said. "You go ahead, Dave. I'll call Mike in, and then he can get the other two who are out there somewhere. No use waking the stage driver or his passenger. Or Kelso, either."

Dave went into the house and on through the hall door into the dining room. When he saw the three-layer chocolate cake on the table, he said, "Looks like you've been busy."

"Might as well be busy as sleep the last few hours of your life," she said cheerfully. "I've got a revolver in the kitchen. They ain't gonna use me the way they done the Meeker women."

As she poured his cup of coffee and cut a piece of cake, he said, "I'll take that up to Miss Morgan."

As he climbed the stairs he could not keep the bitter thought out of his mind that if Sharon did not have the consuming hatred for the Utes that burned so steadily in her, their reunion would have been a different event than it had turned out to be.

Both hands were full, so when he reached the door he tapped his boot against the casing. She asked, "Who's there?"

"Dave," he answered.

She opened the door at once, saying, "I wondered if you were ever coming back."

"I've got cake and coffee," he said. "I didn't think you'd be asleep."

"Good," she said. "I wasn't asleep and I am hungry. I couldn't eat much supper." When he handed the cup and cake plate to her, she asked, "What about you? Have you had yours?"

"Mine's still downstairs."

"Well, go get it," she said. "You might as well eat with me as anybody else."

He went back to the dining room and returned a moment later. She shut the door behind him and pulled up the only chair in the room for him, then she sat down on the bed and began to eat. She was the most amazing woman he had ever known, he told himself, and in spite of the irritation he felt because of the way she had received him early in the evening, he was aware of a new and comforting warmth that came just from being with her. She had always done that to him when they weren't quarreling.

The thought struck him that her hatred for the Utes was like a cancer; if it could be cut out her body would be healthy. But he doubted that it could be. For most people time was a healer, but her hatred of the Indians was as feral as the day she had heard of her Uncle Ben's murder.

She glanced at him, her mouth full of cake. She swallowed, took a drink of coffee, and said, "You're looking at me as if I had three heads. I guess I should have put my hair up and dressed."

He shook his head, smiling. "It's just that you're a beautiful woman and I like to look at you. I had forgotten how beautiful you were."

She bowed. "Thank you, kind sir. I will pay for the compliment shortly, but I must finish this cake first. I wish I was as good a cook as Mrs. Patrick."

"You are," he said. "I can personally testify to that."

"You are as full of blarney as ever," she said. "Maybe that's why I love you."

He hesitated, not sure how much he should tell her about what he had been doing or what they had decided. If she was frightened, she didn't show it. She seemed unconcerned as if she had known all the time he would work it out. She did not act as if they had been apart for nine months, either. This puzzled him more than anything else.

"I guess you'd like to know what we're going to do," he said finally. "We're taking Conway to Gunnison and we'll see that he's jailed. He'll have to stand trial for Johnson's murder."

"Oh honey, that's wonderful." She rose and put her cup and plate down on the bureau top, then went to him and, placing her hands on his cheeks, tipped his head back and kissed him, her lips warm and sweet and eager. Then she drew back and whispered, "I knew you would fix it, and that you wouldn't give Conway to the Indians. Now hurry up and finish eating."

"I can't take all the credit . . ."

"I'll give it to you whether you'll take it or not," she said. "I thought Harlan would give you trouble, but I wasn't worried about Major Leslie. You remember I told you once about how strong you were inside. Well, this is proof of it."

She dropped down on the bed and lay on her back, her gaze on the ceiling, her hands laced under her head. "I've let myself do a lot of dreaming when you were gone. I think someday you'll be in Congress. Or the governor of Colorado and I'll be the first lady."

He finished the cake and coffee and set the dishes on the bureau, then moved to the bed and stood looking down at her. He thought about the time she had told him that marriage was forever, that she would not marry a man unless she could improve him.

"Are you marrying me because of my political future?" he asked. "Or because you're going to make me over into the kind of man you want? Or is it for my money?"

"All three." She laughed and held out her arms to him. "I had forgotten what a delightful idiot you are."

He lay down beside her, not sure he could trust himself, or her, either. She held him hard against her, kissing him with a passion that was like a great wind whirling him along head over heels. Suddenly she pushed him back, whispering, "Sweet Dave, that's enough. It was almost more than enough. I had forgotten how good it was to hold you in my arms again." She pulled his head down and cushioned it with her breast. "Just lie here and let me settle back to earth."

"You think I'll settle back?" he asked. "Or did you know where you were sending me?"

"I knew," she said softly. "Of course I knew. That's how I could tell it was time to quit."

"You're a foolhardy woman to run a risk like that," he said. "Or else you didn't care."

"I guess I didn't really care,' she said. "Not while you had me sailing over the mountain peaks, but I came to earth and now I do."

He lay there while his heart slowed down. The minutes passed and it seemed to him that this was only a short calm before the storm, a moment of peace when he closed his mind against what lay ahead. He dozed for a time until the dawn light began filtering into the darkness, then Sam Leslie's voice aroused him. "Dave, they're coming."

"I'll be right down," he called.

Sharon sat up as he crossed to the window and looked out. A great body of horsemen was moving slowly toward the house. The light was too thin to be sure, but he thought Shavano was the lead rider. There must be fifty of them, he judged, or more.

Sharon said, "What is it?"

He walked back to the bed. "The Indians are coming. I'll go down and talk to them with Leslie. We'll tell them what we're going to do. We won't fight because that would be suicide for all of us, including you and Mrs. Patrick, and we're not going to take Conway to the agency or the Army post because that would result in a fight. But if Shavano refuses to settle for a trial in Gunnison, anything can happen. You stay here. Do you have a pistol?"

"Yes," she whispered.

"If it comes to the worst, use it on yourself," he said. "That would be better for you than having to go through what the Meeker women did."

He kissed her again, then he straightened and stood looking at her for a moment, her eyes wide with terror, her lips parted. He turned and left the room, wondering if he would ever see her again.

13

Leslie was waiting for Dave on the front porch. When Dave joined him, he asked, "Do you have a gun?"

"No."

"Good. This may be touch and go. If you had a gun you might be tempted to use it, and that's all it would take."

"Maybe we ought to see that everybody who's in the house is ready to fight in case we get into trouble."

"My boys are in the bar and they're armed," Leslie said. "So's the stage driver and the passenger, but six men wouldn't do much against a crowd like this."

"Harlan?"

"He's gone. So are the soldiers."

They stepped off the porch and walked toward the approaching Utes. They met a moment later, Shavano and Indian Henry in front. The other braves made a circle around Dave and Leslie. All were armed, most of them with Henry rifles, but several, Shavano included, wore cartridge belts around their waists and revolvers in their holsters.

Shavano was clad in a blue Army officer's uniform. Dave had been told that someone had given the uniform to Shavano at Fort Garland years ago and he had been very careful with it, wearing it only on special occasions. A few of the others wore buckskin, but most of them were in faded blue shirts, bibless overalls, and cowboy hats. Many wore eagle feathers slanting back from their heads.

Shavano said, "How."

Dave and Leslie said, "How," and waited.

Shavano looked past them at the house, then brought his

gaze back to Leslie. He said nothing for a time. Except for his eyes which blinked occasionally, he might have been a bronze statue in a blue suit. He was taller than Ouray had been, and his face was thinner than it had been the last time Dave had seen him. He did not show grief for his son, but there was a kind of haunting, wild gentleness in his face that told Dave he felt the same grief a white father would feel, perhaps more.

There was no sound except from the Indian ponies and a rooster who crowed from somewhere back of the stable. The Utes hadn't come racing in on their horses, whooping and screaming and waving their rifles the way Leslie said they had done at the agency when they'd first heard about Johnson's murder. In a way this sullen silence was more terrifying. Dave did not doubt that a threatening move, a wrong word, a shot from the house would turn them into a screaming, savage mob in a matter of seconds.

"You give Conway to us?" Shavano asked in Spanish.

"No," Leslie said. "We are taking him to Gunnison as soon as we have breakfast. He'll be locked up in jail and he will be tried for the murder of your son."

Dave drew the notebook from his pocket and flipped it open to Kelso's statement. He said, "Young Bucks will have to testify at the trial. We also have the signed statement of the other freighter. He says it was murder."

Dave's Spanish had improved during the months he had been in Arizona and New Mexico and he was sure Shavano understood. He thought he saw a flicker of interest in the chief's dark face. Shavano reached for the notebook and Dave gave it to him. He studied the page of writing, but Dave was sure he could not read, that it was only so much chicken scratching to him.

Presently Shavano handed the notebook to Leslie. "Read it to me," he ordered.

Leslie translated Kelso's statement into Spanish, then gave the notebook back to Dave. A warrior down the line suddenly yelled, "White man God damn. We kill. Papooses. Squaws. Men. Everybody."

Shavano turned his head and said something in the Ute tongue. Dave did not know what it was, but from the tone of his voice, Dave judged he was giving the brave a dressing down. The instant Shavano was done, the warrior whirled his horse out of the line and galloped back the way he had come, whooping with every jump his pony made. He was a young man dressed in buckskin, and now for the first time Dave was aware that few young men were here. Nearly all of the men were middle-aged, as old as Shavano or older. Young Bucks wasn't in the crowd, a discovery that vaguely disturbed Dave.

"Where is agent?" Shavano asked at last.

"He returned to the agency with the soldiers," Leslie said. "He wants you and your men to go back and not bother us when we take Conway to Gunnison."

Dave could not tell from Shavano's inscrutable face what his feelings were. Dave said, "Carl Schurz wants the Utes to be treated like white men. That was why he appointed Ouray to the commission and why he wants each Ute to have a farm that will belong to him. It is why we will take Conway to Gunnison for trial the same as if he had murdered a white man."

"Wano," Shavano said. "You take Conway to Gunnison and we go back to the agency. You turn Conway loose and there will be bad trouble."

"We'll take him to jail," Leslie said. "You'll have to trust us the same as we trust you to go back to the agency."

Dave saw at once that Leslie should not have said this. Probably Shavano's experience with white men had taught him not to trust any of them, not even as good a friend as Sam Leslie was. For a time the chief sat motionless, his dark eyes on Leslie's face, then he said, "We go to agency now." He motioned to Indian Henry. "He goes with you."

Shavano whirled his horse and galloped back the way he had come, the others except Indian Henry stringing out behind him. For a moment Leslie didn't move, but stood staring at the departing Indians, the first sharp rays of the sun touching the ridge to the west.

"We'd better eat and get started as soon as we can," Leslie muttered as he turned toward the house. "Damn it,

I shouldn't have said that about trusting each other. He sure let us know he didn't trust us.''

"Will he take Conway away from us?" Dave asked.

"He won't break his word, and he'll see that the men who were with him return to the agency," Leslie said. "Trouble is the young braves weren't with him."

Dave glanced at him and saw that he was deeply troubled. Dave asked, "Who was the one who rode off?"

"They call him Keno Bill," Leslie said. "He's a bad one. He's an Uncompahgre, all right, but they say he was with the White River Utes during the Milk Creek fracas."

When they reached the house, Leslie stepped into the bar. "Jake, tell Conway to come and get his breakfast. We're taking him to jail in Gunnison. Barney, you and Tug saddle up four horses, the best animals we've got. Mike, you're going with us."

"Now hold on, Major," Collins said. "I've been through enough hell since that damned Conway and Kelso showed up here. I ain't gonna risk my neck for that bastard."

"Your neck is no more valuable than mine or Dave Rand's," Leslie said. "Shavano has promised that if we take Conway to jail to be tried, he will go back to the agency and not bother us. He'll keep his word. Now let's eat breakfast."

Barney and Tug left the house, Jake went back along the hall to bring Conway from the office, but Collins stood motionless, his expression sullen and rebellious. Leslie did no wait to argue, but strode into the dining room where Mrs. Patrick was pouring coffee. Finally Collins shrugged and muttered, "Sure, and no man lives forever." Then he grinned at Dave. "He's a hard man to say no to."

They joined Leslie at the table just as Mrs. Patrick brought a platter of flapjacks from the kitchen. Conway came in with Jake, his heavy-lipped mouth wide in a mocking grin as he sat down across from Leslie.

"Well, Major," Conway said, "all this time I thought you was going to turn me over to the red devils so they could skin me alive, but now Jake says we're going to Gunnison."

"To jail, Conway," Leslie said. "You'll be tried and hanged."

Conway speared a flapjack. "You're just fooling yourself," he said. "That jail won't hold me, Major. No white jury is going to find me guilty. They might even give me a reward for making a good Indian out of a live one." He poured syrup over his flapjack and filled his mouth and chomped loudly, then he pointed his fork at Leslie and added, "I guess you found out you was a white man. That was why you couldn't turn a white man over to . . ."

"You're no white man." Leslie rose, hands on the table as he leaned toward Conway, his face dark with fury. Or if you are, you're a disgrace. Now I'm not going to listen to any more of your lip. Shut up, or by God, I'll knock every one of your teeth down your throat."

"Better do it, Conway," Collins said from the other end of the table. "I seen him get mad at a mule once and he knocked every tooth that mule had right down his throat."

Conway stared at Leslie for a moment as if puzzled by the storm he had provoked, then he shrugged. "All right, all right."

"Hurry up with your breakfast," Leslie said as he dropped back into his chair. "We've got to get started."

Five minutes later the four men rose from the table. When Dave reached the hall, he found that Sharon was waiting for him at at the foot of the stairs. She put her hands on his shoulders, asking, "Are you going now?"

"Right away," he said.

"Will there be trouble?"

"The major doesn't think so," Dave answered. "Shavano gave his word that he would go back to the agency and not bother us."

Her lips curled in contempt. "I wouldn't trust an Indian's word."

That was the other Sharon, the one he didn't like, the one who kept bobbing up when he didn't want to see or hear her. He said, "We've got to get started."

She kissed him, her lips lingering on his. Then she drew back and whispered, "I'll pray for you. Please come back."

"I aim to," he said.

He strode outside, wondering if this was the way it would always be with them. Upstairs their relationship had been as perfect as it could be and he had thought it would be the same when she had told him good-bye. Perhaps he had become oversensitive to her attitude toward the Utes, but it seemed to him she had reached out to destroy the perfection of their relationship, that she could not bear the thought that he might forget how much she despised and hated the Indians.

His saddle was on a big sorrel. He was glad he did not have to ride his bay because the horse needed rest. As soon as he mounted, Leslie handed him a Winchester. He saw that both Leslie and Collins were armed.

"You and Conway take the lead," Leslie said. "Mike and me will bring up the rear."

"What about Indian Henry?" Dave asked.

"I don't give a small damn where he rides," Leslie said irritably. "His being here isn't my idea."

"Let's get moving," Dave said to Conway.

They headed east, the sun a full circle above the mesa ahead of them. Dave glanced at the house and saw that Sharon was on the front porch waving at him. She was holding her robe so that it made a tight fit around her hips; the slanted rays of the sun falling directly upon her so that she looked as if she were illuminated by a very bright light.

He raised a hand in farewell, then turned his head to stare straight ahead. For a little time he continued to see her, so firmly was the image of her slender body impressed upon his mind. Then the image faded.

He was not like Sam Leslie, he thought. Leslie had said that no one would weep for him if he died. Sharon would cry for Dave Rand if he did not return. He thought about this for a time because it seemed so important for a man to be loved. Then he told himself it would be the good Sharon who would miss him, the kind, sweet Sharon who had held him in her arms and kissed him and cushioned his head with her breast. Maybe if he forgot the other Sharon, if he just ignored her, she would go away.

* * *

For a time none of the four white men talked. Indian Henry, who rode between the two pairs of white men, was equally silent. He was a squat, dark-skinned Indian who knew little if any English. Dave could not remember anything about him, but he must have had Shavano's respect or he would not be here. Dave wondered if he planned to go all the way to Gunnison. Probably only to the reservation line, he decided. It might be dangerous for a Ute to show up in Gunnison.

Leslie and Collins rode about twenty yards behind Dave and Conway. Whenever Dave glanced back at them, he had a feeling that Mike Collins was uncomfortable and wished he was anywhere but here. Leslie seemed unaware that anyone was with him. He was plainly anxious, his gaze sweeping the slope ahead of them where the timber met the grass-covered valley. When Dave looked at the fringe of spruce ahead of them, he saw nothing except a few of Leslie's cows that were grazing.

Leslie was worried, but he hadn't said what was bothering him. Dave wondered if he expected an attack by some of the young men like Young Bucks who had not been with Shavano that morning. Or gunfire from the timber that would kill Conway and possibly all of them.

It had always been an excuse with Indians for the chiefs to say they could not control their young men, while all the time they knew what was happening, but Dave couldn't believe Shavano would make such an excuse or that he did not intend to keep his word. Still, it was quite evident that Leslie expected trouble.

For about two miles the road ran almost straight across the valley and up the lower part of the slope. When they reached the trees, the road began to swing in wide loops, a thick growth of spruce on both sides. They were in the timber for another mile. Dave kept one hand on the Winchester so he could snatch it quickly from the boot if he had a sudden need for it, but he did not see or hear anything to indicate that another human was within a mile of them.

Conway apparently was not worried in the slightest. He

was whistling tunelessly until they reached a small park, then he said, "Well, I guess all three of you bastards wanted to see me dead, but you ain't going to. You won't keep me in the Gunnison jail twelve hours. I've got friends in that town." He laughed. "I'll tell you something, Rand. Any other white man would have done the same as I done except an Injun lover like you."

"Shut up," Dave said.

"Why should I?" Conway asked. "Shavano didn't have the guts to fight for me, did he? None of 'em will. I don't owe you or Leslie nothing, so why should I do what you tell me?" He spat into the dust at the edge of the road and wiped his mouth with the back of his hand, then turned his head to grin at Dave. "I suppose old Shavano was fool enough to believe all you told me about standing trial. Well sir, this country is in a hell of a shape when a white man has to go to jail for killing a goddamned stinking Ute . . ."

He stopped, the words dying in his throat. In that instant a horde of mounted Indians erupted from the timber and raced toward the white men, yelling and whooping and holding their rifles above their heads. A shrill sound like the scream of a woman broke out of Conway, then he cried out, "You bastards knew this would happen. You fixed it up with Shavano."

Indian Henry yelled something in Ute and galloped past Dave and Conway. Dave looked back and saw that they were surrounded. He yanked the Winchester from the boot and touched up his horse so that he was ahead of Conway, then stopped. He guessed there were fifty or more Indians in the crowd, all of them young men. Young Bucks was riding directly toward Conway who had pulled his horse to a stop a few feet behind Dave's. Keno Bill was a short distance from Young Bucks.

No one was paying any attention to Indian Henry who was yelling and waving for them to stop. When he saw they weren't going to, he threw his rifle to his shoulder and fired. Then they were on him. Somebody, Dave thought it was Keno Bill, knocked Indian Henry off his horse and sent him rolling, and then like a great wave sweeping across a flat beach, they were all around Dave and Conway, Keno Bill shouting, "We take 'em."

Dave did not know what had happened to Leslie or Collins. He had no time to look around. He shouted, "No. Utes can't take white man."

"Yes, we take 'em," Keno Bill yelled.

Dave rammed the muzzle of his Winchester into Keno Bill's stomach. "I said no. We made a deal with Shavano. We've got to take white man to Gunnison to be tried for killing Johnson."

Dave had never heard so much howling in his life. The Indians were pressing close, their horses whirling and plunging, but above all the other racket Dave heard Conway's frantic, terrified scream, "Don't let 'em have me, Rand. Don't let 'em take me."

At the moment Keno Bill wasn't saying anything with Dave's gun jammed into his stomach, but Young Bucks shouted, "This is him. He kill Johnson. We kill him."

"No," Dave bellowed, shaking his head at Young Bucks. "No. We promised Shavano the white man would be tried for murder."

"Maybe we take you, too," Young Bucks yelled. "We try him. We kill him. You no likem, you vamoose." Young Bucks motioned toward the Cimarron. "You ride like hell over hill."

Then Keno Bill found enough breath to snarl, "White man God damn."

Now, in all this racket and commotion and under the threat of instant death, the thought flashed through Dave's mind that he would not see Sharon alive again, and with it was the second thought that Collins was right when he'd said that Duke Conway was not worth being killed for.

All Dave had to do was to pull his rifle back and say for the Indians to take Conway. But Dave had known the risk when they'd left Leslie's place. He could not in honor do anything different than what he was doing.

Dave kept shaking his head. He shouted, "No. White man put in our charge. We've got to take him to Gunnison."

Young Bucks started to raise his rifle, his dark face alive with hate. Dave did not have time to swing his Winchester to cover Young Bucks. If he tried, Keno Bill would kill him. He wondered what had happened to Leslie and Collins. If he had a little help from either one . . .

He had not been looking at Conway, but now he heard an excited yell from the Indians and realized that Conway was making a run for it. He dug in his spurs and took after Conway who, surprising the Indians, had broken through their ranks.

"No, Conway," Dave yelled. "Come back, you fool."

But Conway wasn't coming back. Hunched low over his horse's neck, he was cracking steel to his mount at every jump.

The Utes' attention had been fixed on Dave, and Conway's unexpected flight had shocked them into momentary immobility. Or maybe Leslie and Collins had done something to hold them. All Dave knew for sure was that one brave had got the jump on him and was between him and Conway. The Indian was bringing his rifle up to his shoulder to shoot the fugitive in the back, and although Dave's sorrel was faster than the Indian's paint, he knew he would not be able to stop the brave from getting off at least one shot.

The Indian was the length of his horse ahead of Dave when he fired. He missed, even as close as he was. Before he had time to jack another shell into the chamber and cock and squeeze the trigger, Dave was close enough to grab the arm nearest to him and pull the Indian off his horse.

The brave fell hard. Dave didn't look back to see if he was hurt or what was happening to Leslie and Collins. He had to get Conway or all three of the whites who were taking him to Gunnison would die, a prospect that meant nothing to Conway who was thinking only of his own escape.

Dave was glad that Leslie had given Conway the poorest horse of the four. Dave's big sorrel was gaining with every step. A moment later he came even with Conway's mount and, reaching out, grabbed the reins.

Conway struck at him, screaming, "Let me go. Let me go."

Dave pulled both horses to a stop. "What are you trying to do?" he demanded. "Get us all killed?"

"You sold me out, didn't you?" Conway shouted. "You made a deal with 'em, didn't you, you and Leslie and that damned Harlan."

"No we didn't," Dave snapped.

He looked back. The Indians were coming on the run, Keno Bill and Young Bucks in the lead. Behind them Mike Collins sat his saddle, his hands in the air. Sam Leslie was on the ground ten feet in front of him. Leslie wasn't moving, but Dave couldn't tell whether he was alive or not.

The Utes crowded around Dave and Conway, Young Bucks striking Conway in the face. Conway raised his fist, then dropped it when Dave called, "Don't do it, Conway." Dave spurred his sorrel in between Young Bucks' pony and Conway's horse, suddenly aware he didn't have his rifle, but he couldn't remember how or when he had lost it.

"We take 'em," Young Bucks said. "We take you, too."

"You can't." Dave looked the Ute in the eyes. "It's like I told you a while ago. We made an agreement with Shavano. We've got to take the white man to Gunnison where he'll be tried."

They weren't yelling now, but Dave found no comfort in the silence. The Indians were sullenly quiet as they milled around. Dave, watching them, thought they were more dangerous now than when they had been making so much noise.

Keno Bill turned and motioned at Collins. He yelled, "You ride over the hill. Ride like hell."

Collins did not need a second order. He whirled his horse and disappeared into the timber. Dave thought: *They're going to kill both of us and they don't want a witness*.

"Don't you savvy what you're doing?" Dave shouted. "You'll be hunted down and hung. All your people will be hurt by what you're doing."

But there was no reasoning with them. They were determined to execute Conway themselves. Probably they knew as well as Dave did that a white jury would not be likely to convict Conway and that he'd be a free man in a matter of days.

Keno Bill prodded Dave with the muzzle of his rifle. He motioned to the south. "Ride."

Mike Collins was gone and Sam Leslie was probably dead and Duke Conway, who was responsible for all the trouble, was sitting his saddle, pale-faced and as jittery as an aspen leaf. Dave could do nothing against fifty Indians, but when Keno Bill prodded him a second time, he lost his temper.

He slapped the rifle barrel to one side and gripped it with both hands. He yanked on the rifle and tumbled Keno Bill off his horse, and then he was on the ground and dropping on top of the Indian, his knees striking the brave in the belly and driving wind out of him.

Keno Bill grunted and drew his knife, but Dave twisted it out of his hand and threw it to one side. He slugged the Indian in the face. That was all. A warrior struck Dave on the head with the barrel of his rifle. He fell sideways onto the grass, thinking that Keno Bill would cut his heart out. But Young Bucks intervened.

"Put 'em on horse," Young Bucks said.

Keno Bill picked up his knife and got to his feet. He glared at Dave, the desire to kill a naked hunger in his eyes, but he made no move to satisfy that hunger. Several braves lifted Dave to his saddle. He did not completely lose consciousness, but for a time he couldn't make his muscles obey his mental orders. He seemed oddly detached, as if he were separated from his body. He clutched the saddle horn, his head wobbling from one side to the other.

Keno Bill spit on him and said, "White man God damn." He turned to his horse and mounted.

Young Bucks and Keno Bill led the way into the timber to the south, dropping into a ravine which led into a deep canyon. One of the Indians led Conway's horse. Another Ute had the reins of Dave's sorrel. He held back while most of the party moved past them and followed Young Bucks and Keno Bill down the ravine.

Presently there were just two braves with Dave. They were about the age of Young Bucks and probably had been Johnson's friends. He could not guess why he was being held back or what they intended to do to him. He looked at one and then the other, but he could not make out the slightest hint of expression in their dark, inscrutable eyes. Certainly there was no trace of mercy.

After several minutes had passed, one of the braves motioned for Dave to ride down the ravine. The rest of the party had almost reached the bottom of the canyon so that Dave caught only occasional glimpses of them through the quaking asps.

Dave's head ached, his lips were dry and cracked, and blood had trickled down his forehead and his right cheek from the blow he had received. He wiped it away and ran the tip of his tongue over his lips, but it was as dry as his lips.

He had the feeling this was a nightmare and he would wake up and find himself in bed. He looked at his fingers and saw the flecks of dried blood that he had wiped off his face. No, this was no nightmare. Every time the sorrel brought a foot down, an explosion of pain in his head threatened to blow off the top of his skull.

They probably intended to kill Conway and then the rest of them would come back and kill him. He told himself again that they didn't know what they were doing or what the results would be, but there was no way he could make them understand. He had tried and he had failed.

Mike Collins would probably leave the country. If he moved fast enough he would be all right, but even if Sam Leslie and Dave lived, they would never be able to prove that they didn't make a deal with Shavano just as Conway had accused him of doing.

When they reached the bottom of the canyon, one of the braves said, "We stop."

Neither of the Indians seemed to be watching him. One dismounted and drank from the small stream that flowed swiftly down the canyon, then the other did the same. Dave could not hear the main party. He stepped down and

stood with a hand on the saddle horn. He had a chance, he
thought, if he moved fast and struck hard.

His captors stood several feet apart, apparently paying
little attention to him. They seemed to be waiting for
something, maybe for the rest to return. One of them saw
a large ant crawling on the ground. He squatted beside it
and, picking up a twig, began to torture it. If they didn't
torture Conway to death, if they would just kill him out-
right, quickly and . . .

He heard the rifle shots, two of them. *Conway was
dead*. They hadn't tortured him after all. The rest would be
back in a little while. If he was going to do anything, he
had better do it now.

One of the braves said something in Ute, and turned to
his horse. Just as he made the turn, Dave lunged at him,
his right fist catching the Indian squarely on the chin. He
went back and down.

Dave whirled toward the one who had been torturing the
ant, but he was too slow. For the second time within the
hour a rifle barrel crushed against his head and he toppled
forward, but this time he had no memory of what happened afterward. He kept falling and falling into what
seemed to be a black pit that had no bottom, and presently
there was only the blackness.

14

Dave came to with the sun shining directly on his face. He crawled into the shade. For what seemed a long time he lay motionless, his eyes closed. His head hurt and every move he made caused it to hurt worse.

For a while he was conscious only of the racking pain that made him sick, then he forced himself to roll over so he could drink from the creek and wash his face.

He heard a woodpecker hammering away back in the timber. A couple of marmots were brown mounds on the rocks above him. From somewhere on up the side of the canyon came the raucous cry of a jay. Slowly the memory of what had happened worked back into his mind. Conway was dead. Dave had taken two beatings and risked his life for the man, and still he was dead. Dave was sure of that as he could be sure of anything.

Slowly Dave got to his feet. The Indians were gone, but his horse was still here. He started toward the sorrel, then the ground began to roll in front of him like the surface of the ocean. He put both hands on the saddle to steady himself and closed his eyes. Later he managed to lift himself into the saddle and then almost fainted as waves of nausea beat at him. Somehow he hung on to consciousness. As soon as he was able, he turned his sorrel up the ravine.

He let the horse pick his path and take his own time. It was all he could do to stay aboard. When he reached the road he would probably find Sam Leslie's body unless Collins had sent a man to get it, but when he reached the park where the Indians had made their appearance, he saw that Sam Leslie was sitting with his back to the trunk of a quakie, battered but very much alive.

Dave rode up to him and slowly and painfully eased out of the saddle. He said, "I thought you were dead, Sam."

"Funny thing," Leslie said. "I thought *you* were dead. Somebody slugged hell out of me and when I came to, you and Conway were gone. So was everybody else."

Dave sat down beside him. "Your horse light out for home?"

"I guess he did. I thought I could walk that far, but I only went about fifty feet and fell on my face. I reckon I fainted."

Dave told him what had happened.

Leslie sat silently through Dave's recital and then said, wearily, "I tried, Dave. Damned if I didn't, and if I'd had some help from Mike Collins, we might have done some good. I dunno, but he sure meant it when he said he wasn't going to get killed saving Conway's life.

"I was behind you and Conway, and most of the Indians were in front of me, so when he made a run for it, you took after him and I got my gun on the Indians. The one who was ahead of you must have been way over on the side. I don't even remember seeing him, but I do remember hearing the shot. Anyhow, I told 'em I'd kill the first one who took after you. They were crazy for Conway's hide, but not so crazy they were going to get shot.

"Well, I held 'em off your back a little while, and all the time they were milling around in front of me and trying to get around behind me. Maybe one of 'em did. I knew I couldn't hold 'em very long. Anyhow, somebody clubbed me and that's all I remember. I've got a hunch it was Collins."

Dave, remembering how Keno Bill had told Collins to ride, thought that Leslie had probably guessed right. He said, "I got it twice and you got it once. We must have the toughest heads on the reservation."

"We've probably got cracked ones," Leslie said. "We'll take it easy till the doc from the agency can look 'em over."

"I guess I should have hunted for Conway's body," Dave said.

"Oh, he's dead, all right," Leslie said, "but chances are they'll tote the body on down the canyon and maybe hide it under some brush. You wouldn't have found it. You know, they didn't fire a shot except the one when Conway tried to run. All they wanted was to give us a hell of a headache and keep us out of trouble."

"If we'd have shot one of them," Dave said, "it might have been different."

"You bet it would," Leslie agreed.

"You figure Shavano broke his word?"

"No. He may have had a hunch this would happen, but he kept his bunch out of the fracas. I doubt there was any way he could have handled Keno Bill's outfit." Leslie paused and felt gingerly of the back of his head. "The way they look at it, they executed a murderer, and I'm not so sure they done wrong."

"Want to try riding behind me?" Dave asked.

"I'll try, but you'd better keep to a slow walk," Leslie said. "My noggin feels like part of it's gone, but I can't find a hole in it anywhere."

"I'm not in favor of a gallop, either," Dave said.

Dave mounted. It took Leslie several attempts before he succeeded in getting aboard. Even after he did, he put his head against Dave's back, his arms tight around Dave's waist. Presently he said, "All right, I think I can make it."

The sun was noon high when they reached the ranch. The men were in the yard. Jake said, "I'll take your horse," as Leslie eased to the ground and Dave followed.

"You can hitch up and roll," Leslie said to the stage driver. "You won't have any trouble with the Indians." He looked around and, not seeing Collins, asked, "Where's Mike?"

"He lit a shuck out of here," Jake said. "Told me he'd save you the trouble of firing him if you got back alive."

Leslie grunted, and then he said, "I'm going to bed. Jake, you light out for the agency and tell Harlan they jumped us and took Conway. Bring the doc back. Me and Dave got cracked heads out of the fracas.''

"Right away," Jake said. "You figure Conway's dead?"

"He's dead, all right," Leslie said, and walked slowly to the house.

Vince Kelso had been standing apart from the others, but now the group broke up and Kelso stood alone, staring at him. Dave did not feel like talking or fighting with him. He started to follow Leslie to the house when Kelso said, "You made a fool out of me last night like you've done before, but it didn't save Conway's life, did it? You made a deal with Shavano to give Conway up to save your hides, didn't you, you and Leslie?"

Sometime during the morning Dave had lost his hat. He looked at Kelso, the sun pouring its noon heat down upon him. He was sick and tired and a sense of failure beat at him. Staring at Kelso, he realized he hated the man for the unfairness of his question.

No one could have done more than he had to save Conway's life. He had certainly taken risks that Kelso would not have taken. If he and Leslie had followed any other course, such as forting up in the house and fighting off the Utes, all of them would be dead. Kelso knew this, and still he was vindictive enough to throw the blame for Conway's killing on Dave.

"No, we didn't make a deal," Dave said, and started toward the house.

He almost reached the porch before he saw Sharon standing in the doorway. She took one step, her gaze on Dave who stopped and stood looking up at her. She was wearing the same gray suit she had worn a year ago when she had ridden the stage into this country. This surprised Dave, for he had not seen her wear it since she had left here with Kelso on her way to Ouray.

He expected her to say she was glad he was back, glad he was alive, for she must have heard from Collins that he was in the hands of the Indians the last Collins had seen of him. But she just stood there looking at him. Scorn was easy to read in her eyes.

"Your luggage ready to bring down?" Kelso asked.

"It's ready," she answered.

"I'll fetch it," he said. "The stage will be leaving as soon as they get hitched up."

He went past her into the house. Dave knew, then. She was leaving with Kelso. If he had given her a ring, she would be taking it off and throwing it at him.

"How could you do it?" she asked.

"Do what?"

"Let them have him. You told me you were taking him to Gunnison to be tried, but all you did was to take him out there for the Indians to torture and murder. Vince says they will skin him alive and then burn him."

She didn't know what had happened and she didn't want to know. There was no use to explain, so he didn't try. He only said, "We couldn't help it."

She shook her head, contempt more than scorn in her eyes now. She said, "The Spartans either won the battle or came home on their shields." She paused, then added, "But you aren't a Spartan, are you?"

She stepped off the porch and took a step past him, then stopped, and for just a moment he saw the woman he loved, the good, sweet Sharon who had held him in her arms and cushioned his head on her breast only a few hours before. She said, "Love is not enough, is it, Dave?"

"No," he said. "It isn't."

She walked on toward the stagecoach, carrying herself proudly in the regal manner he had always admired. He sat down on the porch and watched her, knowing this was the last time he would ever see her.

She did not love Vince Kelso, she had told him once, but she liked him. Now she would marry him and perhaps make him over into the kind of man she could love. There had been a time when he had thought their different attitudes toward the Indians was not important, that once they were away from here, it would not come up any more, but he had never been more wrong about anything in his life.

He thought: *She would rather have had them kill me than for me to come back alive if I couldn't save Conway.*

Kelso came out of the house with Sharon's luggage. He started toward the stagecoach, then slowly turned, unable to resist gloating over his triumph. He said, "I told you a long time ago she was my kind of woman."

"Be happy," Dave said, "and make her happy. You hear?"

Kelso was surprised, for it was not the kind of response he would have made if the situation had been reversed. He frowned, then shrugged and went on to the coach. The horses were hooked up, Sharon's luggage loaded into the boot, and then the driver climbed to the high seat.

Sharon was inside. Kelso paused, looking at Dave as he lifted a hand in a smug gesture of triumph, then he stepped into the coach and closed the door. The driver sent the silk flying out over the horses. It cracked with a pistol-like report, the horses lunged forward, and the wheels began to turn. A moment later the coach was in the road and headed up the slope toward Blue Mesa, the same road Dave had been on with Leslie and Conway and Collins and Indian Henry early that morning. But it had been a different world then.

Dave sat there a long time watching the coach until it disappeared into the timber and there was only the dust to remind him of its passage. He was not even aware that Jake had ridden away to tell Harlan what had happened and to bring back the doc.

Dave's head still ached with the same pounding throbs that threatened to split his skull, but there was another sickness in him now, a sickness of disappointment, of great loss, of seeing a dream disappear in front of his eyes. Sharon could not help herself. He had not realized that before, and so, realizing it now, he could not blame her.

She was right that love was not enough. There must be the spirit of give and take that went with love if a marriage was to last, of trying to understand how the other person felt. But Sharon could not give or compromise because of the hatred that was in her. As painful as the breakup was to him, and he suspected it was to her, it was better this way, or a greater agony would follow.

You make your choices and then you must live by those choices, right or wrong. The best that anyone could do, he thought, was to walk proudly as he journeyed through life. He had not understood what his mother had meant when she talked to him about it a long time ago, but he did now. He had not picked the easy way today, but if he were given a chance to live these last twelve hours over, he would do exactly as he had done.

Dave Rand looked up the road toward the timber. The dust had settled; it was as if it had never been raised.

Wayne D. Overholser has won three Golden Spur awards from the Western Writers of America and has a long list of fine Western titles to his credit. He was born in Pomeroy, Washington, and attended the University of Montana, University of Oregon, and the University of Southern California before becoming a public school teacher and principal in various Oregon communities. He began writing for Western pulp magazines in 1936 and within a couple of years was a regular contributor to Street & Smith's *Western Story* and Fiction House's *Lariat Story Magazine*. *Buckaroo's Code* (1948) was his first Western novel and remains one of his best. In the 1950s and 1960s, having retired from academic work to concentrate on writing, he would publish as many as four books a year under his own name or a pseudonym, most prominently as Joseph Wayne. *The Bitter Night, The Lone Deputy,* and *The Violent Land* are among the finest of the early Overholser titles. He was asked by William MacLeod Raine, that dean among Western writers, to complete his last novel after Raine's death. Some of Overholser's most rewarding novels were actually collaborations with other Western writers: *Colorado Gold* with Chad Merriman and *Showdown at Stony Creek* with Lewis B. Patten. Overholser's Western novels, no matter under what name they have been published, are based on a solid knowledge of the history and customs of the American frontier West, particularly when set in his two favorite Western states, Oregon and Colorado. When it comes to his characters, he writes with skill, an uncommon sensitivity, and a consistently vivid and accurate vision of a way of life unique in human history.